Heart of a Champion

Heart of a Champion

CARL ✦ DEUKER

LITTLE, BROWN AND COMPANY
BOSTON   TORONTO   LONDON

First Edition

The characters and events portrayed in this book are fictitious. Any similarity to real persons, living or dead, is coincidental and not intended by the author.

Library of Congress Cataloging-in-Publication Data

Deuker, Carl.
  Heart of a champion / by Carl Deuker. — 1st ed.
    p. cm.
  Summary: Seth faces a strain on his friendship with Jimmy, who is both a baseball champion and something of an irresponsible fool, when Jimmy is kicked off the team.
  ISBN 0-316-18166-8
  [1. Baseball — Fiction. 2. Friendship — Fiction.] I. Title.
PZ7.D493He   1993
[Fic] — dc20   92-37231

Joy Street Books are published by Little, Brown and Company (Inc.)

10 9 8 7 6 5 4 3 2 1

RRD-VA

Published simultaneously in Canada
by Little, Brown & Company (Canada) Limited

Printed in the U.S.A.

For Anne Mitchell and Marian Mitchell Deuker

The author wishes to thank Ann Rider,
the editor of this book,
for her assistance and encouragement.

Heart of a Champion

Part One

1♦

My father's game was golf. He was great
at it, too. There is a box full of his trophies in our attic.
If he hadn't died, golf would have been my game too. I
would never have played baseball, would never have
been best friends with Jimmy Winter. I'd have heard
about what happened to him while I was hitting a bucket
of balls at Palo Alto Muni to prepare for the high-school
tournament.

But my father did die, and I've spent the last five years
living and breathing baseball. Most of the time Jimmy
Winter has been by my side. No, that's not right. The
right way to say it is I've been by his side.

I was born in San Francisco, but I've lived all my life
in Redwood City, a boring suburb south of the city. My
father was a traveling salesman for IBM. He died ten
years ago, when I was seven. He was in a hotel in Los
Angeles when he had something like a stroke. He called
the lobby for help, but his speech was slurred. The
switchboard operator figured he was drunk and ignored
him. In the morning a maid found him dead. It's a

horrible way to die — alone in a hotel room begging for help, with people thinking you're just some boozer.

People say I look like my father, and I guess I do a little. From old photos I can tell he was tall and thin and had brown hair, like me. But his face was broad and fleshy, and mine is all angles and bones.

My mother says that every once in a while I'll do something small — scratch my head or plop down on a chair — and it will be exactly the way he used to do it. I always feel strange when she tells me stuff like that. His blood is in my veins, but I never got to know him.

The day of my father's funeral our next-door neighbor, Mr. Mongolin, crouched to my level and looked me in the eye. "You're the man of the house now, Seth. You have to take care of your mother."

I remember my throat going tight, and a panicky feeling coming over me. "Yes, sir, I will," I stammered, and I meant it, even though I didn't have a clue how.

My mom must have overheard. She flashed Mongolin a dirty look, grabbed me by the arm, and pulled me to a quiet corner. "Seth Barham, you're a little boy," she said. "You don't have to take care of anyone."

2♦

My mom waited a year before suing the hotel. She told me she waited because it didn't seem right to act like money could replace my father. She said she finally sued because she felt she had to make the people who were responsible *feel* responsible.

The hotel was owned by some huge corporation. They

had a team of lawyers and buckets of money. My mother had one lawyer and no money.

It took four years before the case made it to court. We flew down to L.A. for the trial. One day I was in my sixth-grade classroom at St. Pius diagramming sentences; the next I was on a jet plane with my mother and grandmother.

I thought it would be exciting, but that courtroom was not fun. On a table in front of the jury was a model of a human head. The doctors used it to explain how my father died. I'm not stupid. I knew it wasn't my father's head. But that model looked so real it scared me. And the way the doctors picked sections out, turned them over, pointed to this vein and that artery — I still have nightmares about it.

On the third day of testimony something went wrong and the judge declared a mistrial. Then the corporation offered to settle. We flew back to San Francisco and took a taxi home. My mother wanted to talk with my grandmother, so I was sent outside.

I remember feeling disappointed as I closed the front door. I was back in Redwood City, and it was like nothing had changed. Whenever I'd asked my mother questions about my father, she'd described him as a saint, a perfect husband and father. I don't blame her — what else could she do? But I didn't have a strong sense of who he was. I'd hoped to learn from the trial what he was really like, good and bad. But to the doctors and the lawyers, my father was nothing but bones and blood and tissue. I hadn't learned anything.

I stood on the front lawn that day wondering what to

do, where to go. Guys from St. Pius lived in the neighborhood. I wasn't best friends with any of them, but if I showed up at Briarfield Park I could usually hook up with somebody.

But that day I didn't much feel like seeing guys from the neighborhood. I didn't want to talk about where I'd been. I didn't want to think about that model on the table. So I walked a half-mile to Henry Ford School. I didn't know anybody who went to Henry Ford.

Once I reached the playground I climbed onto a swing, pushed off, and started pumping. When I was soaring, I'd jump out into the sand as far as I could. The whole time I was pretending I was a fighter pilot, one of the Blue Angels, parachuting from a smoking jet. It's a dumb thing for a sixth-grader to do, but that's what I did.

I'd been there about half an hour when I heard a man's voice boom across the playground. "Use your new glove, Jimmy. You need to break it in before the season starts."

"But the new one hurts my hand."

"I said to use the new one."

That was the first time I saw Jimmy.

He was about my age, but a little taller than me, a little stockier, and his hair was maybe a little darker brown than mine. Other than that, we looked alike. Over the years people have sometimes mistaken us for brothers.

The Super Bowl was one week away, but Jimmy was geared up for baseball — and I mean geared up. He had on a Giants cap, jersey, and pants. He wore orange

4

wristbands and black, cleated shoes. He even had flip-up sunglasses.

I had a glove, but baseball had never been my favorite sport. All you did was stand around waiting for something to happen, but nothing much ever did. I hadn't even gone out for Little League.

But watching Jimmy play catch opened my eyes to the game. His arm was loose and free, and as he released the ball, he'd snap his wrist down and through. The ball would cut through the air like a frozen rope and smack into his father's glove. His father would fire it back. While the ball was in the air, Jimmy acted like he didn't know it was coming. But at the last second his glove would flick out and snare it.

Once they'd warmed up, Jimmy's father hit him grounders. Whenever anybody had hit a grounder at me, I'd stabbed at the ball, my eyes half closed, afraid of taking it in the face.

Not Jimmy. He'd glide over — glove down in the dirt — scoop up the ball, and toss it back. Then he'd pound his fist into his glove, ready for the next one.

Jimmy was a better fielder than any player at St. Pius, but listening to his father, you'd have thought he was terrible. "Use two hands! . . . Keep your glove down! . . . Don't let the ball play you!"

A guy at school, Mike Dokes, had a father like that. Mr. Dokes would scream at the refs and coaches during the basketball games. But mostly he screamed at Mike. As I sat on the swing, I wondered whether it was better to have a father like that, or not to have a father at all.

Just then Jimmy's father hit a ball over Jimmy's head

that rolled out toward me. I slipped out of the swing and tossed it back. "I've got an extra glove," Jimmy said, and he fixed me with his fierce green eyes. "You want to play?"

They put me at second base so Jimmy could practice the throw starting a double play. Mr. Winter would hit a grounder to Jimmy. He'd field the ball and — depending on where he was — either fire it or flip it to me on the bag.

After twenty-five grounders or so, Mr. Winter called out, "One more!" Then he smacked a rocket at Jimmy. For the first time, Jimmy backed off and the ball screamed by him.

His father came unglued. "That was a gutless play, a minor leaguer's play! You get a bruise on your chest, and it goes away. But if a run scores because you let a ball get by, that run stays on the scoreboard forever!"

Jimmy's shoulders sagged and the color drained out of his face. I found myself shaking.

"Try it again!" his father yelled.

"Yes, sir," Jimmy answered.

Mr. Winter laced another grounder, even harder than the one before. Jimmy took it off his chest. "That's better!" his father said, nodding.

I looked over at Jimmy. He had to have been in pain, but his eyes were shining with pride.

Mr. Winter pointed his bat at me. "Now it's your turn, son. Just field the ball and throw it to Jimmy. Okay?"

I was terrified waiting for that first grounder, but when the ball came, it was just a little roller. I fielded it okay,

6

but my feet were tangled when I made my throw. The ball flew about twenty feet over Jimmy's head. Instead of going into a rage, Mr. Winter smiled. "Kid," he said, "let's take it one step at a time."

For the next half hour Mr. Winter showed me how to field a ground ball, set my feet, and throw. He didn't yell once, or act bored, or make me feel stupid.

After that he hit Jimmy and me fly balls and pop-ups. It was the same thing again. Mr. Winter got all over Jimmy if he made the slightest mistake. But he never barked at me. He treated me a thousand times better than he treated his own son, which is one of those things that makes no sense at all, but is true anyway.

Finally Mr. Winter called, "That's it boys."

After Jimmy and I had loaded the equipment into the trunk, Mr. Winter opened a cooler he'd pulled from the backseat. He leaned against the car and drank a beer while we sat behind the backstop and split a Coke.

"What do you think of my father?"

It was the one thing I'd hoped Jimmy wouldn't ask, and it was the first thing he said.

I looked at the ground. "He's okay."

Jimmy frowned. "I know what you're thinking. You're thinking he's mean. But he isn't. He wants what's best for me. My dad made it to Triple-A ball. He says that with a harder push from his father, he could have reached the majors. He's giving me that push, and I'm going all the way to the major leagues." Jimmy took a sip of Coke. "What's your father like?" he asked.

"My father is dead."

"Really? How did he die?"

I told him what had happened.

"I can't imagine not having a dad," he said when I'd finished.

"It's not so bad. I've got my mother."

Jimmy picked up a pebble and threw it. "My mom doesn't understand my dad. They argue a lot."

Mr. Winter called out that it was time to go.

Jimmy stood. "What are you doing next Saturday?"

"Nothing much," I said.

"Come here and we can play some more."

"Maybe," I answered.

He started off, but after he'd gone about five steps he turned back. "I'm sorry about what happened to your dad," he said.

3♦

I'd missed a week of school because of the trial, but when I returned nobody asked me where I'd been. I knew they knew, though, because they all went out of their way to be nice to me. Girls who'd hardly talked to me were lending me pencils. Teachers told me I could take my time making up my assignments. But not one person came right out and said he was sorry.

Maybe that's why I thought about Jimmy so much during the week. When Saturday morning rolled around, I headed straight to Henry Ford. I was half a block away when Jimmy started calling my name and waving. It was like we'd been best friends for years.

That day the three of us played pickle, a baserunning game. The guy in the pickle would keep running, back and forth from first to second, second to first, until he was caught and tagged out. Whoever made the tag would take his place.

Jimmy had a quick first step, and he had baseball smarts. I didn't have either. So it always seemed like he took off when I was sure he wasn't running, and like he hugged the bag when I was certain he was going. He stole base after base. Once he slid into me so hard I flipped in the air and landed flat on my back. He didn't apologize or even help me up.

Mr. Winter came over. I figured he was going to give me a hand, but he didn't. "You were out of position, Seth," he said. "You'll get hurt if you don't play right." Then he explained what I should have done.

Later Mr. Winter had us take turns hitting. Jimmy had a pure swing, even then. Every ball was scorched. But hitting the ball hard wasn't enough for Mr. Winter. "Take outside pitches to right," he'd say. "Drive this one up the middle. Turn on fastballs on the inside part of the plate." He had Jimmy using every inch of the field. I should know — I had to chase the balls down.

I'd never been able to hit a baseball well. I figured it was because I'm not real strong. But Mr. Winter told me I was swinging with my arms. "Start with your weight back. As you swing, firm up your left side and drive through the ball with your legs. Line drives and hard ground balls, that's what you want. Fly balls look prettier, but nine times out of ten they end up dying in somebody's glove."

Around four o'clock we stopped. Mr. Winter drank his beer while Jimmy and I had our Cokes. I was tired,

9

but it was a good tired feeling — until Jimmy started in.

"Listen to my father," he said. "Listen and you'll learn a whole lot really fast."

"I listen," I said.

Jimmy shook his head. "Not hard enough. You've got to pay more attention. He knows everything about baseball."

"Your father isn't God," I snapped.

After that we sat in silence until Mr. Winter called that it was time for Jimmy to leave.

Jimmy stood. "I'll see you tomorrow, won't I?"

There was something desperate about the way he asked.

"Yeah," I said, "I'll be here."

4♦

The next day I was at Henry Ford at noon sharp, and so was Jimmy. I was looking forward to a long afternoon playing baseball. But that was Super Bowl Sunday, and Mr. Winter had a hundred-dollar bet on the game. We'd hardly started when he called it quits.

"Can Seth at least come over?" Jimmy asked.

"Fine by me," his father answered.

"I have to check with my mom," I said.

"You can call from our house," Jimmy said.

"Tell her I'll give you a ride home," Mr. Winter added.

Jimmy lived on Massachusetts Avenue in a house exactly like mine. That may sound weird, but there must be a thousand homes in Redwood City exactly like mine.

After I called my mother, Jimmy pulled two peanut-butter sandwiches out of the refrigerator. "My mom made these this morning. She goes out whenever my dad watches football. She says he gets too loud."

Mr. Winter came in for beer. "You boys going to watch the game with me?"

Jimmy shook his head. "I'm going to show Seth my baseball stuff." He looked at me. "Unless you want to watch the game."

"No," I said. "I'd rather look at your stuff."

Jimmy had the same room in his house that I had in mine, first door down the hall on the right. But nothing else was the same.

My room was boring. I didn't know it until I saw Jimmy's, but it was. My walls were white; my bedspread was white; my curtains were white. I had a stupid picture of Mount Shasta above my bed.

Jimmy had pennants of baseball teams on the ceiling. His bedspread had the logo of the San Francisco Giants on it. The design on the carpet was of a baseball diamond. The walls were covered with posters of ballplayers.

I stared, my mouth open. "Who are these guys?"

If he had been anybody else, I probably wouldn't have asked. But you can tell if a guy is going to make you feel dumb, even if you don't know him much. Jimmy wasn't that kind of guy.

Jimmy pointed them out one at a time. "That's Willie Mays. He did it all. He hit home runs, hit for average, stole bases, and played a great center field. Next to Mays is Juan Marichal. He had a high leg kick and a mean screwball. Opposite Marichal is Willie McCovey. In the

11

seventh game of the 1962 World Series, ..." Jimmy circled his room telling me stories about each of the players.

From his desk I picked up a photograph of an old-time ballplayer. I thought the guy looked stupid with his tiny glove and his baggy uniform. I laughed. "Who's this?"

I'll never forget the look on Jimmy's face as he grabbed the picture out of my hand. "That's Honus Wagner. He was the greatest shortstop ever. He had a .329 lifetime batting average. He signed a contract in 1908 for $10,000 a year, and played twenty-one years without asking for a raise." Jimmy paused. "I'm going to be like Honus Wagner."

He plopped onto the floor and pulled out a huge stack of tattered, dirty baseball cards from the nightstand. I sat down next to him. "Who do you think was better, Stan Musial or Ted Williams?" he asked.

"I don't know," I answered, which was true enough, since I'd barely heard of either of them.

Jimmy held out Musial's card to me. "A lot of people think Williams was, but I don't. Musial hustled more singles into doubles, more doubles into triples. And look what he hit in 1957." Jimmy pointed to a number on the back of the card. "He was thirty-six years old, but he should have won the MVP award that year."

Jimmy talked baseball the whole afternoon. Earned run averages, slugging percentages, walks-to-strikeouts ratios. It was all new to me. But I wasn't bored. They say that baseball is like a fever, and that once you catch it, you never recover. That day I caught it.

When I looked at the clock, it was five-fifteen. I'd told

my mother I'd be home by five. "I've got to go," I said.

Jimmy picked out a dozen of the baseball cards he'd spread over the floor. "You can have these if you want."

"Thanks," I said, and as I took those cards out of his hand I could feel how hard it was for Jimmy to give them away.

In the living room Mr. Winter was stretched out on the sofa, a beer in his hand and a slew of empties on the floor.

"Dad, Seth's got to go home now."

Mr. Winter groaned. "Can't he wait until the game's over?"

I looked at Jimmy. I was already late.

"Dad," Jimmy insisted, "you said you'd take him home."

Driving to my house, Mr. Winter kept spinning the radio dial trying to get the game. He was speeding, too, and hardly slowed down at stop signs.

"You can let me off here," I said once he reached my block. I was barely out the door before he sped off. I didn't even have time to thank him.

The whole week I went back and forth between being eager to see Jimmy again and being afraid to see his father. But when Saturday rolled around and Mr. Winter saw me, he smiled. "You look a little sleepy, Seth. A game of pepper will wake you up."

5♦

I'd been playing baseball with Jimmy and his father every weekend for about a month when my mother noticed I wasn't taking my glove along.

"Mine's too small," I explained. "I use Jimmy's old one."

"Seth," she said a little angrily, "we aren't poor." So after dinner we drove to Five Points Sports. A Wilson glove was on sale. "It's okay," the salesman said. "But if your son is a serious baseball player, I'd recommend this Rawlings." He held up a burgundy-colored model that cost twice as much.

My mother turned to me. "Are you a serious baseball player?"

I nodded.

She looked at the price tag again, frowned, then broke into a smile. "You're just like your father. He always had to have the best, too." She turned back to the salesman. "We'll take the Rawlings. And a couple of baseballs, and a bat."

The salesman tried to talk me into a light bat, but I went for one like Jimmy's.

Before we reached the checkout counter my mother asked if I needed anything else. I'd seen a Giants jersey like the one Jimmy had worn. And they had sweatpants and caps and wristbands and rubber-cleated shoes. I'd even spotted the flip-up sunglasses. By the cash register was a packet of team pennants like the ones Jimmy had hanging in his room.

"Not really," I answered.

She could tell I was holding back. "Here's twenty dollars. But you're not getting any more."

I grabbed the pennants, the cap, and the wristbands.

Before I got into bed that night, I spent ten minutes

14

rubbing saddle soap into my new glove. After that I lay on my bed and pounded my baseball into the pocket again and again. That's what Jimmy told me he did every night. He said all the major leaguers did the same thing. And it worked. With every throw I could feel the leather softening up, the pocket beginning to form.

I finally fell asleep, but I didn't dream about baseball. Instead, I dreamed I was playing golf on a bright, sunny day. In the dream I pulled a seven-iron from my bag, took an easy practice swing, and then hit the ball. It flew up and up, high against the blue sky, cleared a sand trap, bit as it landed on the green, and settled in no more than ten feet from the pin.

But the golf shot isn't why I remember the dream. I remember it because off to the side of the fairway, almost hidden by a eucalyptus tree, stood my father. He didn't say anything to me, and I didn't say anything to him. But he was watching me.

6♦

Jimmy told me about Little League sign-ups. He'd made the major leagues the year before. He played shortstop and batted third for the Woodside Plaza Merchants. He didn't have to try out, but I did.

He had it worked out. I'd get assigned to his team, play second base. We'd be a great double-play combo. He'd bat third and lead the league in hitting and runs batted in. I'd bat second and lead in runs scored. Our team would win the title.

It sounded great to me.

15

On the day of tryouts, there were probably one hundred guys at Red Morton Park. Some man took my name, pinned a number on my back, and asked how old I was and whether I wanted to play infield or outfield.

"I'm twelve," I said. "And I want to play infield."

"Over there."

They called numbers one by one. Each guy took five ground balls — every one a little harder than the one before. The last ball was really stroked. I watched about ten guys before my number was called.

My hands were shaking — that's how nervous I was. The first ball was a simple two-hopper, but I bobbled it. The next two I handled okay, but I got a bad jump on the fourth and the ball slipped through. I could see the man make a mark on his clipboard. I had to field the last ball cleanly — I had to.

The coach swung. The ball exploded off the bat. I froze — unsure whether to step forward and try to take it off my shoe tops, or to back up and field it on the bounce. The ball short-hopped me, skidded off the heel of my glove, and nailed me square in my right eye.

The coach hustled out. "You okay?"

"Yeah, I'm fine."

I had my head down, trying to hide my face, but he made me look up. Then he grimaced. "That eye needs an ice pack. Your parents might even want a doctor to look at it."

"But what about my tryout?" I asked as he led me off the field. "I've got to be on the Woodside Plaza Merchants."

He patted me on the back. "Don't worry. We'll assign

you to a team. Your eye comes first.''

He had me call home, and my mother picked me up about fifteen minutes later. By the time we reached our house, I could open my eye only halfway, and I had the worst headache of my life.

Sunday morning my eye was swollen shut. I didn't want to go, but I forced myself to walk over to Henry Ford. Jimmy's face fell when I told him what had happened. ''Did you tell them you have to be on the Woodside Plaza Merchants?''

''Yeah,'' I said, ''but I don't think it's going to work.''

Mr. Winter came over. ''That's a nasty shiner, Seth. What happened?''

I told the story again. Mr. Winter listened, then turned to Jimmy. ''Well, son, let's get to it. It won't be as much fun without Seth, but you can still get in some practice.''

On Wednesday team assignments were posted. My mother drove me to the Rec Center. My eye was still a little swollen, so I had trouble finding my name on that long, white sheet of paper. When I finally found it, I was crushed. They'd stuck me on the Eng's Palace Mets, a minor-league team.

That night I moped through dinner.

''Look, Seth,'' my mother finally said. ''I know you want to be on the same team as your friend. But Jimmy has been playing for years. You've only been playing a few months. You can't expect to be as good as he is, not without a lot of practice.''

I slumped down in my chair. ''I know. But how am

17

I going to get practice? Nobody else on the block plays baseball. Jimmy's got his father, but —'' I stopped cold. The words had spilled out.

We both sat perfectly still for a long moment. It's a moment we have every once in a while, when both of us feel my father's absence. I never know when those moments are going to come. If I did, I'd stop them. Because I hate them. I hate the way my mother raises her chin and bites down on her jaw, and I hate the way my own heart pounds. It's like we're both paralyzed, like we both want to say something, but there is absolutely nothing to say.

Finally I started clearing the dishes from the table. "It's okay, Mom," I said once I got my hands in the soapy water. "I'll think of something. And the minors won't be so bad."

7♦

After school the next day, I grabbed my glove, my bat, and my ball and shuffled into the backyard. I started by working on my batting stroke. I swung over and over, making sure I kept my head down and the bat level. But after twenty-five swings I stopped. Mr. Winter said if you swing too many times, you swing too hard and end up with bad habits.

I plopped down under our cherry tree, feeling defeated. I wanted to be a good fielder, but how could I get better without somebody to hit balls to me?

I was about to go back inside when an idea came to me. Tennis players hit the ball against a wall for practice.

18

I couldn't throw a hardball against the back of the house, but I could throw a rubber ball. It wouldn't be exactly right, but it would be better than nothing.

I scrounged around in the garage until I found a rubber ball I'd gotten in my Christmas stocking but had never used. My scheme worked pretty well. If I whipped the ball on a fly against the house, it would ricochet back giving me practice with grounders. If I bounced the ball, it would return as a line drive or a pop-up. I could angle the throws to practice going right and left.

After a while I started aiming at the spot where the house and the ground met. That way I wouldn't know whether to expect a grounder or a line drive. I'd have to be ready for anything, like in a real game.

Our lawn was a little ragged, and that meant bad hops. At the time those bad hops made me mad. I'd have fielded ten or twelve in a row without an error, and then the ball would catch a hole in the lawn and go off my glove breaking my streak. But that uneven grass taught me to keep my glove down and my eye on the ball.

When my mother came home from work, she heard the ball pounding against the house and came to the backyard to investigate. "Does that work?" she asked.

"Yeah," I said. "It's okay."

I followed her eyes as she stared at the back of the house. There were dozens of black smudges where the ball had hit the wall. I expected her to tell me to quit, but she didn't. "At the end of the summer you'll have to paint that section" was all she said.

We ate dinner about half an hour later. Once we'd finished, she told me to let the dishes soak. "I'll throw you some grounders with a real baseball, if you'd like.''

"You don't have to," I said.

"I'd like to," she answered. "Your old mom could use some exercise."

She threw me grounders for ten minutes or so. I'd field them and roll them back to her. "Throw it as hard as you can," I told her, and she got some zip on them.

My mother threw me grounders every night during baseball season, and during the next season too. And she would have kept doing it, even when I was in high school, if I'd wanted.

When your father dies, people want to feel sorry for you, they want to say you've missed out. And maybe I have missed out on some things. But lots of guys have fathers who have never thrown them a ground ball in their lives. They say they're too busy, that they have to work. My mother worked full-time as a clerk for San Mateo County, and she cooked and cleaned and kept house and all that stuff. But she found time for me.

8♦

One Saturday Jimmy asked me to go with him and his father to a Giants game. "They're playing the Padres, and it's cap night, too."

I asked my mother. "Let me call Mr. Winter and get a few details," she said.

I'd never been to a major-league game, and as she talked with Mr. Winter I was afraid there'd be some reason why I couldn't go. But when she hung up, she smiled. "Have fun."

20

My mother never drove fast, but on the way to the game Mr. Winter roared past the other cars on the Bayshore Freeway. I kept expecting a cop to stop us, but none did.

When we reached Candlestick, Mr. Winter parked in the first lot. He looked at the signposts. "P-eleven. I'm counting on you boys to remember that."

We found the right entrance, gave our tickets to the usher. Inside, a little man was passing out Giants caps. I stuck mine on my head.

I'll never forget entering a major-league park for the first time. The field seemed so big, the chalk so white, the grass so green. And the thousands and thousands of seats, filling with fans, buzzing with excitement and tension! Bits of baseball conversation floated by. Radios were tuned to the pregame show. This was the real thing, the big show. Looking down on the field, I dreamed of being out there myself. It was a crazy dream for a guy who hadn't even made the majors in Little League, but I dreamed it anyway.

As soon as we were settled, Mr. Winter stood. "I'm going to get myself a beer before the game starts. You boys want some hot dogs and Coke?" I handed him the money my mother had given me for treats, but he handed it right back to me.

In the early innings I tried to talk to Jimmy, but he barely answered. He was leaning toward his father so he could hear the explanations Mr. Winter gave for almost every play. Jimmy's face was tight and twisted, like he was in a math class and wasn't understanding what the teacher was saying. By the top of the third I gave up

21

even trying to talk. The Giants were behind 4–0, and that didn't help my mood either.

In the fifth Mr. Winter got himself another beer and us more hot dogs. The night had turned cold. I was glad my mother had made me bring a jacket.

By the bottom of the sixth, the Giants still hadn't scored a run, and some teenagers behind us started booing them. "Fair-weather fans," Mr. Winter said, looking over his shoulder. "They're the worst."

In the top of the seventh, the Padres leadoff hitter smacked a hard grounder down the third-base line. Kevin Mitchell made a nice stop behind the bag, but threw the ball away. Maybe that rattled Dave Dravecky, the Giants hurler, because on the next pitch he gave up a two-run homer to Benito Santiago. The hitter after that walked, and the guy after him doubled. By the time the top of the seventh was over, the Padres led 8–0.

We stood for the seventh-inning stretch. Mr. Winter bought himself another beer. "C'mon, you can do it," he yelled as the leadoff hitter stepped in.

The teenagers behind us laughed. "Yeah, you can do it," one of them yelled. "You can strike out, you piece of crap!"

Mr. Winter faced around. "Watch your language!"

As soon as Mr. Winter turned back the whole bunch razzed him. "Oooooo, Mr. Tough Guy," they mocked.

Mr. Winter pretended not to hear, but he was mad. He didn't clap, not even when the Giants rallied for four runs and loaded the bases with two down for Will Clark. The whole place was rocking. Jimmy and I yelled and stomped our feet. The count went full; everyone was standing. The Padre pitcher wound up, delivered. Clark swung . . . and missed. Around us people picked up their stuff and headed for the exits.

As the Giants took the field in the top of the eighth, the high-school kids really ripped into them. And "crap" was about the nicest word they used.

Finally Mr. Winter couldn't take any more. He wheeled around to say something, but as he did he knocked his beer onto Jimmy and me. "Can't you hold your booze, old man?" one of the teenagers called down.

"Why you . . ." Mr. Winter started to climb over the seat. I really think he would have gone after them if an usher hadn't come up. The usher talked to the fans around us, then made the teenagers leave.

We sat, totally silent, through the bottom of the eighth. After the third out Mr. Winter told us to pack up our stuff. "I want to beat the traffic."

"We're at P-eleven," I said in the parking lot.

"D-eleven," Mr. Winter snarled.

"No, it's P-eleven. Isn't it, Jimmy?"

"It's P-eleven, Dad."

"Both of you shut up!"

I don't know how Jimmy felt, but I was close to tears. My mother never told me to shut up. She just didn't talk that way.

By the time we found the car and drove home, it was after eleven. My mother made me hot chocolate and had me tell her about the game. I pretended I'd had a great time.

I didn't want to bring up the high-school kids, but she

23

smelled the beer on my coat, so I had to explain what had happened. She didn't say anything, or seem angry, though she did make me shower.

The next morning at breakfast she gave me the news. "You're not going to any more games with Mr. Winter."

"Why?" I asked.

For a long time she wouldn't tell me, but I kept after her. Finally, she said she didn't want me in a car with a man who'd been drinking. I told her that Mr. Winter had only had three beers, and that most men at the ballpark drank beer, but she wouldn't back down.

The whole thing came up one more time — with Jimmy. "My father wasn't drunk at the game," he said, his green eyes flashing, as we sat off by ourselves sipping Cokes that Saturday.

"Who said he was?" I answered.

Jimmy stared at me. "You didn't say it, but I know you were thinking it."

"I wasn't thinking it."

Jimmy looked up. "Good, because he wasn't." He paused. I could feel the anger go out of him. "My dad feels bad about yelling at you. He won't ever say he's sorry. He'd never do that. But he feels bad. I know he does."

9♦

Once Little League started, Jimmy and I couldn't meet at Henry Ford. His team played on Tuesday night and Saturday afternoon. Mine played on

Wednesday and Sunday, so it didn't work out. We still saw each other, though, because we'd go to each other's games whenever we could.

The major leagues played at Kiwanis Field. They had permanent bleachers, dugouts, outfield fences with the distances marked. Groundskeepers chalked the foul lines and the batter's box before every game. They dragged the infield to pick up loose rocks, and on hot days they watered to keep the dust down. The major leaguers had full uniforms — caps, jerseys, pants, socks.

The minors were different. We played at Ben Franklin School. No bleachers, no dugouts, no benches. They put the lines down and dragged the infield at the start of the season, and that was it for the year. Even the outfield was second-rate. Left and center had good, deep fences. But about fifty feet behind the infield in right was a sloping bank covered with bushes. A lazy fly ball could reach that bank. They couldn't give a home run for such a measly hit, so any ball that reached the bank was a ground-rule double.

On Tuesdays and Saturdays I'd go to Kiwanis Field and watch Jimmy play. It should have been fun, but it wasn't. Mr. Winter would go berserk whenever any call went against Jimmy. "That was no strike! . . . He was safe! . . . Are you blind, ump, or are you just stupid?" There were other red-faced fathers at the game, but Mr. Winter screamed loudest and longest. I wondered how Jimmy felt hearing his dad screaming.

That season I measured myself against Jimmy. If he got two hits on Saturday, then I wanted three on Sunday.

If he drove in a run Tuesday, then I wanted two RBIs on Wednesday. When he had a big day it would pump me up. But sometimes it worked the other way. If he'd gone 0 for 4, I'd get it in my head that I was going to have a bad game. In baseball, if you think negative, negative is what you get.

Jimmy didn't have many bad games. So chasing him made me the star of Eng's Palace Mets. That, and the short bank in right field.

Because of Mr. Winter's coaching, I was good at going to the opposite field. Fly balls to right that should have been easy outs would plop down in the bushes on the bank and I'd be standing at second. They were Mickey Mouse doubles, but nobody could have told me that.

At the start of the season, my mother took a picture of me in uniform, bat cocked, tough-guy look on my face. I glued that picture to a piece of cardboard. After every game I'd go home and write down my stats in a notebook I kept in my drawer. At the end of the year I planned to make a baseball card of myself — at bats, hits, runs, RBIs, the whole thing.

Then, the last week of the season, magic struck. The phone rang — I'd been called up by the Woodside Plaza Merchants, Jimmy's team. Only one game remained in the season, but that didn't matter. I'd made the majors.

Jimmy was almost as happy as I was. "I told you," he kept saying. "Didn't I say they'd call you up?"

I was sky-high the whole week. I didn't crash until I got to the park and discovered I wasn't in the starting lineup.

26

I spent that game on the far corner of the bench, waiting. When Woodside Plaza was up, Jimmy would talk to me. But I could barely answer — the lump in my throat was that big. I kept looking at the coach, wondering if I'd ever get in.

In the bottom of the fifth, he pointed toward me. "Steve, grab a bat. You're pinch-hitting for the pitcher."

I looked around. "Me?"

"Yeah, you. Get up there."

I grabbed my bat and raced to the on-deck circle. "Good luck!" Jimmy said as I went by.

While I was on deck, I tried to time the pitcher. He seemed fast, so I decided I'd better choke up, even though Mr. Winter didn't like it. The batter hit a couple of foul balls to right, then struck out.

It was my turn — my first at bat in the major leagues. My heart was thumping. I scratched a little hole for myself deep in the batter's box, brought the bat back — elbows pointed down — and faced the mound.

I'll never forget that first pitch. One second the ball was in his hand, the next instant it was in the catcher's mitt. "Strike one!" the umpire called.

I swallowed, stepped out. I went over what Mr. Winter had said. "Pick up the ball right as it leaves the pitcher's hand." Again the pitcher wound up and delivered.

"Strike two!" the umpire called.

I pounded the bat on the plate. *I'm not going to strike out looking,* I told myself. *No matter what, I'm going to take a hack at it.*

But the final strike was like the first two. The ball was by me before I could pull the trigger.

27

"That's okay," Jimmy said when I returned to the bench. "Steve Cannon is the fastest pitcher in the league. He strikes out almost everybody."

The next hitter bounced back to the box. Jimmy jumped up, grabbed his glove, and took his position at shortstop. I looked to the coach, but he didn't motion me to take the field. My Little League career was over.

That night I took out the notebook I'd used to keep my stats from my games with Eng's Palace Mets. I looked at my high batting average, the RBIs, the doubles. I couldn't believe how dumb I'd been, planning to make a baseball card of myself, thinking that because I could hit in the minors I was a good ballplayer. What a joke! I ripped that notebook to shreds.

I was feeling real sorry for myself, like what had happened to me was the worst thing that had ever happened to anybody. Then, the very next Saturday, Jimmy showed up at Henry Ford without his father.

We played catch and three flies up and hit grounders to each other. But it wasn't until we were finished and were sitting on the grass that he told me what was up. "My father moved out last night," he said. "My parents are going to get a divorce."

My mouth dropped open. "Why?" I managed.

He grimaced. "It's kind of complicated. My mother wants him to do stuff he doesn't want to do."

I wanted to ask what, but I didn't have the guts.

Once I got home, I told my mother.

She surprised me. "Divorce isn't the end of the world, Seth. Jimmy will still see his father."

"Mom," I said, "you don't understand. It won't be
28

the same. Jimmy won't have his father around to play ball and stuff. It's the worst thing that could have happened."

She looked at me like I was missing something that was right in front of my face. For a few seconds I couldn't figure out what it was. Then I understood. I walked down the hall and into my room. I felt ashamed, ashamed of forgetting about my own father.

10✦

School had ended, Little League was over, but Jimmy and I still played baseball through the month of July. Other guys hung out around Henry Ford, so most days we could get up a game. Jimmy always arranged it so that we played on the same team. If somebody objected, Jimmy would shut him up. "Seth and me are going to be a great double-play combo at Woodside High," he'd say. "We've got to practice together."

Jimmy was all smiles those days, but he was real jumpy, too. If a car pulled into the parking lot, he would always look over. I could see the hope in his eyes, but it was never his father. Never.

As the weeks rolled by, the two of us did get better as a double-play combination. We had the feel for each other; we both seemed to know what the other guy was going to do. And at the plate I was getting more than my share of base hits. My batting average was better than lots of guys who had played in the majors in Little League.

I figured on playing baseball all summer. But in

29

August guys started wearing their 49ers jerseys and bringing footballs. By the time school started, Jimmy and I were the only guys still playing baseball.

We'd play catch, then a little pepper. Jimmy would hit me grounders; then I'd hit him grounders. The last thing we did was to throw batting practice to each other. When we were done, we'd lie on the grass and shoot the breeze.

Mostly we'd talk about high-school baseball and what it could lead to. Or maybe I should say Jimmy would talk about it. "A lot of guys get drafted right out of high school," he said. "You spend two, three years in the minors, and then you get your shot at the big leagues. I'm going to be one of those guys, Seth. You wait and see."

Like Jimmy, I fantasized about being a major leaguer. But I would never have told anyone. Steve Cannon had done more than blown the ball right by me. He'd blown a hole in my self-confidence, too.

I don't think a day would go by when I didn't think about that strikeout. I'd be doing something, anything, and then, out of nowhere, the whole at bat would come back to me, like a black cloud I couldn't get out from under.

That's why I asked Jimmy to start pitching hard to me — as hard as he could — during batting practice.

Most of the time you use batting practice to work on things you want to become automatic. Things like bunting and going to the opposite field with fastballs away. It's easier to practice the little things if the pitches are maybe 80 percent of full speed. But working on little things makes sense only if you've got the big things down. If I couldn't get around on a big-time heater, I was going nowhere on the diamond.

When I told Jimmy I wanted him to throw his hardest, he wasn't crazy about it. "I'm no pitcher. What if I hit you in the head?"

"I'll get out of the way. Just throw hard."

He shrugged. "If that's what you want. But you're crazy."

He was wild at first. His first ten pitches were way outside. But then he started getting some over the plate. And I couldn't touch them. Every one was by me before I could get the bat around. Jimmy thought it was a great joke. "Call me Nolan Ryan!" he screamed after I'd whiffed about fifteen in a row. "The Express."

When we finished, we sat on the grass and he started talking for the millionth time about what a great double-play combination we were going to be.

"Why don't you cut it," I growled.

"What's eating you?" he asked.

I told him straight out. "You're going to play Babe Ruth and high-school ball, Jimmy. But I'm going to get cut."

"What are you talking about? Why would you get cut?"

That's how he was. If he wanted something to be true, then it was true.

"In case you haven't noticed," I said sarcastically, "I can't hit a fastball."

I watched my words sink in. For a long time he didn't say anything. Finally his face turned serious. "You'll

31

hit. We'll keep practicing until you do. That's a promise, Seth.''

The next Saturday Jimmy gave me a gift, a new bat. It's the only time in my life anybody other than my mother or grandmother gave me something out of the blue. The bat was thirty-two inches long, but it weighed only twenty-eight ounces. "With a bat like this," he said, "you'll be able to get around on a fastball better. Second basemen don't have to hit for power. Make contact and you'll be all right. And don't feel bad about the bat being light. Lots of major leaguers use light bats.''

He was trying to make it easy for me to switch to a light bat and not feel like a wimp. He didn't have to worry. I would have swung balsa wood if it meant I'd hit better.

I didn't pound the ball that day, not by a long shot. All I managed were a few grounders toward second. But I hit the ball, and that was more than I'd done before. Way more.

Jimmy slapped me on the back when we finished. From the way he acted, you'd have thought I was ripping line drives into the outfield gaps.

The truth is I felt like I had been.

11♦

All through autumn I'd go to the backyard every afternoon and pound the ball against the wall to keep my fielding sharp. On weekends Jimmy would pitch to me, as hard as he could, for as long as he could. Sometimes he'd pitch for so long I'd feel guilty. "Your turn," I'd say. But if he had any life in his arm, he'd keep going. "You need the practice more than I do, you bum!"

He could call me that, and I didn't care, because I was getting better. Sometimes Jimmy even had to jump out of the way of a line drive I'd sent right back up the middle.

The day after Christmas Jimmy told me his father had come by on Christmas Day. "He says he's going to sign up for counseling. That's what my mother has always wanted."

"Great," I said. "Maybe your parents will, you know . . ."

He finished the sentence for me. "Get back together." He pulled some grass out of the ground. "If he does it, sure."

"He said he would, didn't he?"

"Yeah," Jimmy answered, his voice tight.

I poked him in the ribs. "Come on, Jimmy. Be happy."

He looked at me and managed a smile.

12◆

This next thing that happened is a little weird, and I'm ashamed of it. It should never have happened. All I can say is that both Jimmy and I were thirteen years old, and that John Tustin was a lot older.

We were at Henry Ford playing three flies up on a Sunday in late January. Jimmy had caught his third fly ball and was running in to take the bat when Tustin showed up.

Tustin lived on my block. I knew who he was, but since he was sixteen or seventeen years old, I'd never hung out with him. Actually, I'd always been afraid of him, though he'd never done anything to me. There was just something about him.

That day he wanted to play ball with us. It seemed like an okay idea. One more guy would make the game better. Besides, when you're in seventh grade, it's hard to get rid of a high-school kid. If we told him he couldn't play, he might have taken our stuff or pushed us around.

Jimmy was up, but since Tustin was older, Jimmy held out the bat. "As soon as one of us catches three, then we get to hit," he told Tustin.

Tustin yanked the bat from Jimmy. "I know how to play."

Right away we knew we'd made a mistake. Tustin tossed the ball too high, and he didn't keep his eye on it. He missed half the time, and the balls he hit were grounders.

After Tustin had swung two dozen times, neither Jimmy nor I had a catch, and it didn't look like we'd ever get one. "Why don't we play one fly up?" Jimmy called to him.

Tustin glared out. "I can hit the ball," he screamed. He took a ferocious swing and missed. It would have been funny except we were both scared.

Tustin tossed the ball and swung again. This time he did connect solidly, only he pulled the ball out of the park and into the backyard of one of the houses behind Henry Ford.

We peered over the fence for a few seconds. "I guess it's lost," Jimmy said. "I've got to go home anyway."

"Me, too," I chimed in.

"Don't be in such a hurry," Tustin said. "I want to show you guys something."

"Some other time," Jimmy said. "My mom wants me home."

Tustin stared him down. "What do you mean? I've watched you guys lots of times. You play here for hours." He grinned. "You'll like what I've got to show you."

I looked at Jimmy and he looked at me. We didn't really have anywhere to go or anything to do. Besides, we didn't have a clue as to how to get rid of Tustin.

We hid our gear behind the backstop and followed him up Goodwin Avenue to Stulsaft Park. There are no baseball fields or anything up there. It's more like a forest with hiking trails and cliffs and a little creek.

Tustin led us up one of the trails. About every fifty yards either Jimmy or I would ask him where we were going.

"Just shut up," he finally hissed.

About a half-mile up the trail, he pulled back some bushes and pointed. "Through there."

Jimmy and I ducked in; Tustin followed. When he let the bushes go, they snapped into place.

We were in a small clearing. On the far side was a shack made of old planks of wood. Inside were some old, rusty wire chairs and a mattress. Tustin smiled. "I bring all my girlfriends here."

Only once had I seen Tustin with a girl.

Jimmy and I sat in the old chairs. Tustin lay down on the mattress. "You want a cigarette?"

Jimmy shook his head.

Tustin held out the package toward me. "How about you, Seth?"

Right here is where I don't understand myself. I'd never smoked, never wanted to smoke. What did I care about Tustin? Jimmy had turned him down cold. I should have done the same thing. I should have stuck with my friend. But I didn't. I took the cigarette.

Tustin reached behind him, opened up an old box, and pulled out a six-pack of Budweisers. He twisted the top off one and handed the bottle to me. "Thanks," I said. He tried to hand one to Jimmy, but Jimmy wouldn't take it.

"Suit yourself," Tustin said. "It just means more for Seth and me." He raised his bottle to his mouth and chugged about half of it. He wiped his mouth, grinned. "This sure beats the hell out of playing baseball."

I sipped my beer. It tasted bitter and warm.

"So is this what you wanted to show us?" Jimmy said, challengingly. "Some old shack?"

Tustin scowled. He chugged the rest of his beer, then reached into the box again. This time he pulled out some magazines and tossed them toward us. "Feast your eyes."

I was in seventh grade. So it's not like I wasn't interested in sex. But Tustin's magazines were so totally sick
36

they creeped me out. I could tell Jimmy felt the same.

"Pretty hot, aren't they?" Tustin said, reaching around for another beer.

Neither Jimmy nor I answered.

"You know what I do sometimes?" Tustin went on. "Sometimes, I come up here in the afternoon and take off my clothes so that I'm nice and cool and comfortable. Then I lie back on this mattress and drink a few beers and flip through those magazines." He paused. "You guys feel like doing that?"

Jimmy stood. "Get up, Seth, we're getting out of here."

I stood. Jimmy headed across the clearing. As I started to follow, Tustin grabbed hold of my arm. I tried to shake free, but Tustin's grip was strong.

"Let him go!" Jimmy said.

"He doesn't have to go just because you're going," Tustin shot back.

"He's going because he wants to go!" Jimmy yelled. "Don't you, Seth?"

They both were staring at me. I could hardly speak.

"I want to go," I finally stammered.

Tustin held me for a second before he shoved me away. "Get out of here! Both of you! But don't tell anybody about this place or I'll make you pay!"

We staggered across the clearing, scrambled through the bushes, stumbled onto the path. Then we both ran as fast as we could until we were back at Henry Ford.

I half expected our gear to have been stolen, but it was still there. My baseball glove, my bat, my ball — none of them ever looked better.

We didn't play catch or hit ground balls. We just sat behind the backstop. Jimmy squeezed the handle of his bat and took some half-swings. I did the same. The wind was blowing through the high branches of the trees.

"Let's make a pact," Jimmy finally said. "You and me. No cigarettes, no drinking, no drugs, no girls. Just baseball. Okay?"

"Okay," I said.

It sounds corny, but we sort of touched bats then, to seal the agreement.

Whenever I think about that day, one thing always bothers me: what would have happened if Jimmy hadn't been there? I'd like to think I would have left, that I was just about ready to get up, and that Jimmy just beat me to it. But maybe that's a lie. Maybe I wouldn't have had the courage to leave. I hadn't wanted the cigarette, but I'd smoked it. I hadn't wanted the beer, but I'd drunk it. Maybe Jimmy saved me. Maybe without him I would have done anything Tustin wanted me to do.

13♦

I kept expecting Mr. Winter to show up at Henry Ford with Jimmy, but he never did. Jimmy never mentioned anything about his father moving back into the house, either. It didn't take a genius to figure out something had gone wrong.

One weekend toward the end of February the rain fell so hard Jimmy and I were stuck playing Wiffle ball in my garage. I propped up a milk crate on top of an old box. Any ball that went into the crate was a strike. On

38

the opposite wall we drew lines. If a ball hit above the highest line it was a homer, the next highest was a triple, and so on.

There's no way to throw a Wiffle ball fast. It flutters, like a knuckleball. You have to stay back on the ball and adjust your swing as you're swinging. Jimmy's bat speed didn't do him any good.

The first game we played, I trounced him 11–3. Not that it should have been any big deal. But Jimmy didn't like losing. "Let's play again," he said as soon as he struck out to end the game.

I pasted him 8–2, then 7–4. "Another game," he insisted both times immediately after the final out.

"Come on, Jimmy," I said after I'd beaten him again, "let's do something else." But he wouldn't quit.

We played Saturday and Sunday. Sometime in there winning the games became as important to me as it was to him. I could feel how badly he wanted to beat me, and that made me want to make sure he didn't.

They were stupid Wiffle-ball games in the garage, but we played like they were the World Series. We crashed into the wall to take away doubles and triples; we argued about balls that hit on the line; we shredded our elbows trying to throw rainbow curves and hard sliders. We must have played twenty games that weekend, and I won them all. When Jimmy left Sunday we were hardly talking.

The next weekend came up sunny, and I was glad of it. I didn't want to spend any more time cooped up in a dark garage playing Wiffle ball and being mad. Besides, Babe Ruth tryouts were coming up. I needed practice hitting fastballs, not Wiffle balls.

39

But being out in the sunshine hadn't taken the fire out of Jimmy. He didn't say anything, but that whole afternoon he didn't seem right.

It was during my batting practice that it happened. The pitcher's mound at Henry Ford was muddy from the rain. Jimmy had trouble with his follow-though, and I suppose that slowed down his fastball a touch.

Anyway, I caught a pitch on the screws and sent a rocket to left. I kept waiting for the ball to bounce, but instead of coming down, it soared over the fence. "A dinger!" I screamed, and I threw both my arms up in the air. I did a little dance, tipped my cap to imaginary fans in the bleachers, flexed my biceps.

Jimmy didn't laugh. "One lucky swing doesn't make you Babe Ruth," he yelled.

"What's eating you?" I asked.

"Nothing's eating me. Just get back in the box."

I took my spot in the batter's box, dug in a little, then nodded that I was ready.

But I wasn't ready — not for what came. It was a fastball, high and tight, right at my head, that sent me sprawling into the dirt. The ball smacked into the backstop, and I was up and yelling.

"You trying to kill me?"

"It was an accident."

"That was no accident!"

Jimmy glared. "Maybe it wasn't. Maybe you need to know what you'll get if you show up a pitcher."

"We're practicing, Jimmy. And you're not a pitcher."

"I'm telling you, Seth. Don't show me up."

"And I'm telling you, don't throw at my head."

"Get back in the box."

I wiped the dirt off my pants, picked up my bat, stepped back in. I scowled at him, but the truth is my knees felt like Jell-O. I'd never had a beanball come that close, and it had taken the heart right out of me. I could feel the ball against the side of my head. I could feel it splintering the bones, bruising the tissues, bursting the blood vessels. My mind went back to the model of the human head at the trial. Jimmy's pitch could have killed me. Maybe he didn't know it, but I did. It took every ounce of courage I possessed to stay in the box.

The next day neither of us mentioned what had happened, but neither of us had forgotten it. Jimmy kept the ball out over the plate. After a while my knees firmed up and I started swinging normally. I even nailed another home run, but I didn't act any differently than when I'd dribbled a grounder up the first-base line.

"Nice hitting," Jimmy said when I was done, and I knew he meant it.

"Thanks," I replied.

We walked in silence toward the street.

"I'm sorry about yesterday," Jimmy said when we reached his block. "I shouldn't have thrown at you."

"Forget it," I said. "I shouldn't have been showboating either."

14♦

I was anxious for Babe Ruth tryouts. I thought I could hit. But I wouldn't really *know* until I'd made solid contact against a real pitcher.

The day of tryouts I was incredibly nervous. While Jimmy and I played catch to warm up, I couldn't keep from peeking at the other guys around us. They seemed bigger, stronger, faster, better than me. "Don't worry," Jimmy said when the coach called us in. "None of these guys has picked up a ball all winter."

I felt better once we started infield practice. I handled the grounders and pop-ups they hit me okay. Next came situation practice. The coach would yell out something like, "Runner at third, one out," before hitting a grounder or a pop-up or a fly ball. A lot of guys would field the ball okay, but then not know what base to throw to. I always knew what to do when the ball came to me.

The last part of the tryout was batting practice. Waiting for my turn, the whole Steve Cannon nightmare came back to me. I was afraid I'd get in the box and not be able to touch anything. But the fastballs they threw me were about what Jimmy had been throwing, maybe a little slower. I never did relax, but that's not the worst thing when you're batting. Tension keeps you sharp. I got two dozen pitches, and I handled them pretty well.

After the last guy hit, the coach spoke. "Listen up, gentlemen. I wish you could all play. But with Little League, adult softball, American Legion — well, there just aren't enough fields. Some of you won't make this team. I'm sorry. I really am." He paused. "I'll post the roster at the Rec Center office by noon tomorrow. Thanks for trying out."

As we walked home, Jimmy told me I was dead-certain to make the team. "Don't sweat it."

But I did sweat it. That night I kept waking up every

hour or so. I relived every moment of the tryout, trying to find a place where I'd screwed up, but I couldn't.

I didn't eat the next morning. I tried to kill time watching television, but it was no use. So I slipped into the backyard and pounded the ball off the wall. I must have gone into a trance, because the next thing I knew my mother was at the back door. "It's almost twelve-thirty. I'll give you a ride over to the Rec Center."

Neither of us spoke on the way. My mother pulled into the lot and waited while I went inside. From across the room the words jumped at me. "Redwood City Babe Ruth Reds." I looked down the list, my heart thumping. I spotted Jimmy's name at the bottom, but I couldn't find my own. I felt a numbness come over me. It wasn't fair. I looked again. And there it was, at the top, Seth Barham, the first name. I'd looked right past it.

On the ride home I told my mother how lucky I was to make the team, how if they'd thrown me fastballs like Steve Cannon's I would have been cut. When we pulled up in front of the house, she turned off the engine, then looked at me. "Seth, I don't want to hear any more about luck. The way you've practiced baseball, the hours you've put into it — you've been exactly like your father was with golf. Exactly. He called it *working* at his game. That's what you've done. You have *worked* your way onto that team, so be proud of yourself."

Later that night, when I was tossing my baseball into my glove, I thought again about what my mother had said, and a question came to me. My mother was in the front room reading. "What is it, Seth?" she asked when she saw me in the doorway.

43

"Nothing, really. Only this afternoon you said my father had to work real hard at golf. I guess I always thought the game came easy to him, that he was a natural."

She laughed then, a sad laugh. "According to your father, he was anything but. As a matter of fact, the only thing we argued about were the hours and hours he spent on his golf game. He used to say that he had to practice because he was a lousy golfer. The best lousy golfer in the world, he said, but still a lousy golfer. That never made any sense to me. Does it make sense to you?"

I thought for a moment. "Not too much," I said.

My mother smiled. "Well, if you ever figure it out, tell me. I'd like to know."

15✦

Mr. Loffler coached the Redwood City Reds. He was a nice enough guy but he didn't know a lot about baseball. That didn't bother me. Just being on the team made me happy. I had a full uniform, and I'd be playing on fields with fresh chalk lines, real fences. "I want you boys to have fun," Mr. Loffler said. That's what I intended to do.

The only hitch was Jimmy. Every time Loffler gave us a tip, Jimmy would interrupt. "That's wrong. My father says . . ." At the final practice before our first game, Loffler had us turning double plays. He positioned us maybe two steps from where Mr. Winter would have had us. No big deal. During the game we could have moved to our old spots and Loffler wouldn't have no-

44

ticed. But Jimmy wouldn't let it go. "We should be in a step and over a step," he insisted. "That's how my father would have us do it."

Loffler had heard enough. He glowered at Jimmy. "Son, I'm getting tired of hearing about what your father would do. Especially since I never see him. I'd be delighted to have him give up some of his time to help me out. If he wants, he can coach the team. Believe me, I'll find something else to do. But until he shows his face, you'll do things my way. Understand?"

Jimmy's eyes bore into Loffler.

"Do you understand?" Loffler repeated.

"Yeah, I understand," Jimmy answered, still staring.

Walking home after practice, I told Jimmy that Loffler might have been on to something. "I know he was riding you, but maybe your father could help coach. That way —"

He stopped me cold. "Seth, you don't know what you're talking about, so why don't you shut up."

He'd never jumped on me before, not like that. I should have told him off, but I was too stunned to say anything.

16♦

The afternoon of our first game was typical for April in California — warm and sunny. My mother didn't go to many of my games, but she drove Jimmy and me to the park for that one. When we got out of the car, she called me back. "I'm proud of you," she whispered, and then she gave me a kiss.

I was jittery through warm-ups, and I didn't even think about my mother. But when the ump yelled "Play ball!" and I hustled out to second base, I looked into the stands. There were only about thirty people in the bleachers, so it was easy to catch her eye. She smiled and waved.

That's when I spotted Mr. Winter. He was sitting about two rows behind my mother, his arm around a young woman who was definitely not Jimmy's mother.

I looked over to Jimmy. The bill of his cap was pulled down; his eyes were glued on the batter at home plate. But if I'd seen his father, then Jimmy had seen him too.

Like a lot of first games, this one started out weird. Our pitcher, Jeff Cole, walked the first two San Carlos Mariners on eight pitches, then struck out the next guy with three fastballs down the heart of the plate. Their cleanup hitter took two mighty swings and came up empty both times. Then, on the 0-2 pitch, he checked his swing and dumped a little flare out of my reach into short right. A weak hit, but the run scored. The next batter crushed Cole's first pitch — but he smacked it right at Jimmy. Jimmy gloved it, and his throw doubled the runner off first.

I was hitting in the two spot, so I ran in, grabbed my bat, and hustled to the on-deck circle. I hadn't felt too nervous in the field, but once I started swinging my bat, I found myself kind of belching and gasping for air. I forgot about my mother, Mr. Winter, his girlfriend, Jimmy. All I was thinking about was myself.

Our leadoff hitter, Joey Reichler, grounded out on the second pitch. "Batter up!" the ump yelled, and just like that I was standing at the plate for my first at bat in Babe Ruth.

Fastball — that's what I was looking for, but that's what I was afraid of, too — afraid that I wouldn't be able to get around on it, that I'd strike out like I had against Cannon. And a fastball is what I got — knee-high and down the middle. I pulled the trigger.

As long as I live, I'll never forget the feeling that went through the bat and into my hands and up my arms to my brain. I'd caught the ball squarely and ripped a hard grounder up the middle and into center field. I had a hit, and it had come off a fastball. As I rounded first base, I took a deep breath. When I exhaled, a great calm came over me. For the first time I knew, I really *knew,* I could hit Babe Ruth pitching.

There was no time to celebrate, though. I had to get my head back into the game. Harley Jaspar nubbed a 2-1 pitch toward the mound. I took off and slid hard into second, but there was no play on me. The pitcher had taken the sure out at first.

That brought Jimmy up in a perfect situation to get us both off to a great start. A hit would give me my first run scored, and it would give Jimmy his first RBI. All in the first inning of the first game.

As Jimmy took a final practice cut, his father rose out of the bleachers. "Come on, son!" he shouted. "You can do it."

It was an okay thing to say, but the way he said it wasn't okay. He was too loud and the words ran together. Mr. Winter was drunk. I don't know how I knew it, but I knew it. And so did everybody in the park.

Jimmy peered out at the pitcher. The first pitch was a curve, a foot outside, the kind of pitch Jimmy never bit on. But this time he lunged at it for strike one. "Jimmy! Jimmy! Jimmy!" his father yelled. "Look 'em over." The next pitch was in the same place, which is smart pitching. Jimmy lunged again, which is definitely not smart hitting. "What kind of a swing is that?" Mr. Winter bellowed. Jimmy stepped out, adjusted his helmet, stepped back in. The pitcher stretched, delivered — a fastball a foot outside. Jimmy couldn't have hit it with a pole, but he waved at it anyway. Strike three. "Ahhh!" his father groaned, throwing his hands up.

All through the game Mr. Winter yelled advice to Jimmy. And all through the game I kept looking for a good time to tell Jimmy to play ball and forget about his father. I never found it, which shouldn't be any big surprise. When would it ever be a good time to tell a guy to forget about his father?

The game settled into a pitchers' duel. San Carlos managed another run in the fifth on an error by Jimmy, a stolen base, and an RBI double. Their pitcher had us eating out of his hand. We scratched out a hit here and there, but we never had more than one base runner in any inning. As we came in for our last at bat, Coach Loffler clapped his hands. "C'mon, guys, we can get them!" But even he didn't sound like he had much hope.

Our first two guys went down on infield pop-ups. That brought me to the plate. The pitcher got two quick strikes on me, one on a foul and the other on a lousy call by the ump. I felt like dead meat up there. The parents in

48

the bleachers started packing up to go home.

But I lucked out. I don't know whether their pitcher was tiring, or whether he was trying to be too tricky, but he threw me a fat change-up. I couldn't have ordered an easier pitch to hit. I ripped a line shot into the gap in left center and took second base standing up. That brought the guys on the bench back to life, and it made the parents sit down again.

I bobbed around out at second, trying to rattle the pitcher. He stretched, looked back at me, wheeled, and fired to Jaspar. He overthrew it, and the ball sailed inside, grazing Jaspar on the arm. Harley rubbed it off and trotted down to first.

Two on, two out, with Jimmy at the plate. Their pitcher looked sick to his stomach, and everything had happened so quickly no reliever was ready. The pitcher stretched. I bluffed off second. He kind of flinched, and then he started to throw home but stopped. "Balk!" the umpire yelled, and he motioned Jaspar and me to move up a base.

Now we were really cooking. A game that looked lost was coming back to us. A single from Jimmy would tie it. "Just a little bingo," I shouted. "That's all we need."

At that moment I spotted Mr. Winter directly behind home plate. His fingers were curled around the Cyclone fence, and he had his mouth right up against it. "Come on, son," he boomed. "Show them what you're really made of."

The ump called time, took off his mask. "Back up a couple of steps, buddy," he said.

"I'll stand where I want to," Mr. Winter barked.

"You're not going to stand there, pal. A foul ball could break your fingers."

"Move back, Dad," Jimmy said. "Please."

Everybody in the park watched Jimmy's father let go of the fence and back up a couple of steps.

"Is this okay?" he snarled.

The ump didn't answer. "Play ball," he called as he pulled his mask back down.

With his father hovering behind him, Jimmy struck out on three pitches. I don't think he came within a foot of the ball on any of them.

As Jimmy and I were packing up our gear after the game, Mr. Winter came to the bench, the woman right with him. "I'll give you a ride home, son."

Jimmy stuffed his cleats into his bag. "That's okay, Dad. I'll catch a ride with Seth."

Mr. Winter's eyes went mean. I was afraid he'd do something crazy, maybe grab for Jimmy or something. But his girlfriend tugged on his arm. In the end, the two of them walked away.

At the next practice Jimmy's fielding stunk and so did his hitting. Loffler yelled at him, but Jimmy shrugged instead of getting fired up.

"I have to quit the team," Jimmy told me afterward as we were walking home. "My mom is going to rent out the house. We're moving in with my grandparents in Belmont."

My chest tightened. I couldn't imagine not seeing Jimmy anymore. "You can't move," I said at last.

"We have to. You saw my father. He's running

around with his new girlfriend. My mother can't stand it, and neither can I."

"But what good is moving to Belmont? You still might see him."

He sighed. "You might as well know everything. Two nights ago my father pounded on the door about midnight. When my mother opened it a crack, he shoved his way in. He screamed that she had a guy with her, and that he was going to kill them both. He tore through the house looking in all the rooms, even in the closets. Then he grabbed her and started shaking her. She has bruises on both her arms."

We'd reached the corner where he turned off. We both knew that our days of hanging out together were over, and neither of us wanted them to end. Finally Jimmy spoke. "Well, there's one good thing. Next year I'll be able to play on the Belmont Braves. They've won the Babe Ruth title four straight years, you know."

I shook my head. "No, I didn't know."

"Well, they have," Jimmy said. He paused. "Look, Seth, I've really got to go. There's lots of packing to do."

"Maybe I'll see you around," I said.

"Yeah, maybe," he answered.

If we'd been girls, we would have exchanged addresses. Belmont is only eight miles from Redwood City. We could have figured out some way to meet. But we didn't. I watched him head up his block. Then I headed home.

Part Two

1♦

Jimmy was gone. But in a weird sort of way he wasn't. It was like he'd reached into my life and given me a good shaking, like he'd taken my eyelids and pulled them wide open and let the light in. There was no going back to the old ways.

Take television. That first Saturday in May when I knew Jimmy wouldn't be at the park, I turned the tube on. After ten minutes I was out of the house. It was stupid to sit indoors when there was a baseball diamond where a game might be going.

And the kind of competitor I was — that was different, too. Before Jimmy, if somebody started goofing off and ruining a game, I wouldn't have said anything. I hadn't cared enough to argue with anybody about anything.

Jimmy had made me care.

I found that out in July after Babe Ruth season ended, when I had my run-in with Greg Dayley.

When you're in a league, the umpires make the close

calls and keep guys from fighting. I'd had a good time in Babe Ruth, even without Jimmy, even though we didn't win many games. I hit over .300, and played second base well enough to dream again about being a major leaguer.

But Babe Ruth season ended in late June. I still wanted to play ball, so every day that summer I'd pack up my gear, head over to Henry Ford, and get a game going with whoever else showed up. That's where I ran into Dayley.

He was big and strong and mean. Everyone said that in a fight he once pounded a guy's head into a wall and knocked him unconscious.

It was always the same thing. After the first couple of innings, Dayley would start cheating. He'd claim to be safe when he was really out, or he'd say he checked his swing when everybody knew he'd swung through. Pretty soon other guys started cheating, and then we had big arguments and the games got ugly.

I didn't do anything about Dayley for a couple of weeks because I kept hoping he'd stop coming. I guess I was afraid of him, too. But every day I got madder and madder.

One day in mid-July, Dayley rifled a shot up the alley in right center. Our right fielder cut it off and threw a nice one-hopper to me. Dayley was out by ten feet, but when I put the tag on him, he grabbed my arm, pulled the ball out of my glove, and threw it on the ground. "Safe!" he screamed. "You dropped the ball!"

He stood on the bag, a stupid grin on his face. He was

sucking the joy right out of the game, and laughing in our faces while he did it.

"Stop being an idiot," I said.

It took a while for the words to sink into his thick skull. "What did you call me?"

A crazy courage swelled up in me. "I called you an idiot."

"Oh, yeah?"

He came off the base, stuck his foot behind my leg, and shoved me hard. I fell backward and landed in a heap. "Have a nice trip?" he leered, looming over me, fists clenched.

I remember the sweat dripping down my forehead and into my eyes. I wasn't sure what I was going to do, but I knew I couldn't let Dayley run that baseball field. Not without a fight.

The other guys were behind me; I felt it. They liked baseball. Maybe not as much as I did, maybe not enough to take on Dayley, but they wanted to play ball. They were counting on me to make Dayley play right or quit.

I scrambled to my feet, picked up the ball, and tagged Dayley on the arm. "You're out, Dayley," I said. "You're off the bag. You were out before, for interference. But now you're out again. My team is up."

I strode by him toward home plate.

"I'm not out!" Dayley roared. "And your team is not up!"

For a second the rest of the guys stayed frozen. Their eyes went from Dayley . . . to me . . . to Dayley.

Then one of the guys on my team ran in, and then another, and another. The players on Dayley's team picked up their gloves and hustled out to their positions in the field. Dayley was stunned. When he finally understood the game was going on as if he weren't there, he charged in and grabbed a bat from the on-deck circle. His eyes were on fire. I thought he was going to beat my brains out, but after what seemed like forever he turned and hurled the bat into left field.

"This is a stupid game," he bellowed. He raced out to the pitcher's mound, yanked the ball out of the pitcher's hand, and threw it as far as he could. Then he stormed off the field. He never showed up again.

After that I was the leader on the diamond. I did the things Jimmy had done. If the teams were unfair, I moved a guy or two to even them. If there was a close play, I made the call. One day I was late, and when I got to the park the game hadn't started. "We were waiting for you, Seth," Noah Ahlstrom said. "We knew you'd be coming."

Every single night I'd rub saddle soap into my glove before I went to sleep. Then I'd smack a ball into the pocket over and over while I dreamed about being a major-league ballplayer. Finally I'd stick the ball in the pocket and tie a rope tight around the glove. As I stuck it up on the shelf in my closet, I used to think that Jimmy was probably doing the same thing at that same moment. And I wondered if he ever thought of me.

2♦

At school I'd changed too. Up until eighth grade I was basically a C student. But the first quarter that year I had all A's and B's.

"This is wonderful!" my mother said when she saw my report card. "Why didn't you tell me you were doing so well?"

It sounds stupid, but I didn't tell her because I didn't realize I had been. That report card was a shock to me too. And on the next report card my grades were even higher.

Back then I dreamed up all sorts of crazy explanations. One thing for sure is that I didn't think my good grades had anything to do with Jimmy. But I do now.

Jimmy taught me to concentrate. It was on baseball: on ground balls and line drives, on fastballs and curveballs, on knowing when to go for a double play and when to take the sure out at first. But it was concentration.

And that's what school takes. I didn't study any harder. "Stay alive." That's what Jimmy said on the diamond. I stayed alive in the classroom.

My favorite subject was English, mainly because Mr. Dravus didn't make us read Newbery Medal books like my other English teachers had. All we had to do was turn in one book report every month.

I read nothing but baseball books. I started out with a book on Honus Wagner; then I read one about Jackie Robinson. After that they went by like a blur. I know I read about Mays, Mantle, Ruth, Cobb, Gehrig, Williams, Musial — all the greats. Those books were real eye-openers.

56

Coaches make it seem like all the great players are hardworking and dedicated. But that's not true. Some of the best baseball players — like Ruth and Mantle — drank and smoked and stayed up all hours of the night. But they were still great. Lots of players in the minors work hard, real hard, but never amount to anything.

The truth is that some guys can hit a curveball and some guys can't, some guys can run down fly balls and some guys can't, some guys can drive a ninety-mile-an-hour fastball out of the park, and some guys can't touch it, not in a million years, no matter how much they practice.

To be great you've got to have it. You can screw up and waste it. But if you don't have it in the first place, there's nothing you can do to get it. Nothing.

3♦

I hadn't forgotten Jimmy. But I'd given up on him, given up on him like you give up on a twisting foul ball down the line that you know you can never reach no matter how hard you run. Jimmy lived in Belmont; I lived in Redwood City. Eight miles — but he might as well have lived on the moon.

Then, right before Babe Ruth was ready to start up again, I got a phone call. "This is Jimmy Winter," he said. "Remember me?"

For a moment I was speechless. I absolutely couldn't make a word come out of my mouth.

"Seth? Are you there?"

"Yeah, Jimmy," I said finally. "I'm here."

"Listen. How would you like to play on the Belmont Braves this year?"

My head was spinning. I was so excited to hear his voice, I could barely follow what he was saying.

"Who wouldn't?" I finally stammered.

"Here's all you have to do. Come to Belmont High Saturday and pick up a registration form. But instead of putting your address down, put down my grandparents' address. Have your mother sign it, and mail it in."

I tried to think. The whole conversation was so fast, so unexpected. "Won't someone notice we don't have the same last name?"

He snickered at that. "Nobody checks. Half the guys on the team don't live in Belmont."

"Really?"

"I'm not kidding."

After I hung up, I headed straight into the living room and told my mother about Jimmy's plan. When I finished, she looked at me quizzically. "Run that by me again," she said.

I went through it more slowly. As I spoke, her face soured. "Wouldn't you call that cheating?" she asked.

"Not exactly."

"What would you call it?"

"It's just bending the rules."

She took a deep breath. "Seth, let me tell you a story about your father. The first week we moved into this house, Mr. Mongolin invited him to play golf. He said he had a good time. But when Mr. Mongolin wanted to play again, your father wouldn't go. I asked him why. It turned out your father had seen Mr. Mongolin kick his

58

golf ball out from behind a tree. No big deal, really. Just kind of bending the rules. But it was enough to keep your father from ever playing with him.''

"Oh, Mom," I said, "this is differ —"

She cut me off. "Is it, Seth?"

When I called Jimmy back, he got angry. "Did you tell your mother lots of guys do this?" ·

"Yeah, sure. I told her everything. Look, it's hopeless. I know my mother. She won't give in."

There was a long pause.

"Your mother is a total bitch," Jimmy finally said.

I flushed all over, then went icy cold. I know I should have made him take it back. But I didn't. I talked to him a few more minutes before hanging up.

That phone call happened more than three years ago. Some things you try to remember, and the harder you try, the more impossible it becomes. And then there are things you want to forget — like that phone call — and they never go away.

4♦

Just before Babe Ruth season began, a counselor from Woodside High came to St. Pius. Most of the kids at St. Pius were going to Catholic high schools, but there were about ten others beside me who went to the music room to register.

Once we were all seated, the counselor stood. "Woodside is a fine high school," he said. "One of the best in the country. And we are hoping, we are expecting, that each and every one of you — through your talent and

59

hard work — will make it even better. These next four years might just be the best years of your life. Make the most of them.''

We had already filled out the basic forms — name, address, phone number, that sort of stuff — a week earlier. This meeting was to nail down our schedules. The counselor went into the back office and called us to him one by one.

I'll never forget sitting in the music room, trying to make myself believe that I was actually going to be in high school in four months. I was sick of St. Pius, sick of being treated as if I were still a little kid. But I wasn't sure I was ready for Woodside, either. I was afraid it would be too hard, that I wouldn't be able to cut it.

My turn finally came. The counselor had me sit on a metal folding chair. He looked at my transcript and then smiled broadly. ''This is going to be easy. You've put together a fine academic record, Seth. A fine academic record. Your grades are so good, in fact, that you qualify for our honors program. That covers the core subjects — English, mathematics, history, and science.'' He paused. ''P.E. is required by the state, so all I need to know is what foreign language you want to take, and then we're done.''

I was stunned. An honors program! I didn't belong in any honors program. He must have seen the fear in my eyes.

''Don't you want to be in the program?'' he asked.

I shook my head. ''Those classes are too hard. I'm no brain. The kids in there are all going to be smarter than I am. I'll flunk.''

He leaned back in his chair. "I don't see why you feel that way, Seth. You've done well at St. Pius; you'll do well at Woodside. And in four years you'll go off to Cal Berkeley or UCLA and you'll do fine there, too."

I remembered a clip I'd seen about UCLA on ESPN at halftime of a basketball game. The lecture halls were like huge movie theaters. The library had millions of books, and the students were so serious. Their hands were flying across the keyboards of laptop computers or filling yellow notepads with tiny writing. I couldn't picture myself studying late, studying Shakespeare or about the atmosphere of Saturn. I didn't want anything to do with any honors program. I felt as if I were drowning.

"I don't want to go to UCLA or any school like that," I managed at last. "I'm not sure I want to go to college at all. Couldn't I take easier classes, like business math or something? I don't have to be in the honors program, do I?"

He breathed in, then exhaled loudly. "No, Seth, you don't have to be in the honors program." He shook his head. "I'll tell you what I'll do. I'll make out two schedules for you. One honors, one a little softer. You go home, talk it over with your mother. See what she says. Tomorrow morning sign one of these schedules and drop it in the mail. Okay?"

I nodded. "Okay."

I put off talking to my mother until I was almost ready to go to sleep. I guess I expected her to tell me I had to take the honors classes. I was all set for a big argument, but she threw the decision right back at me. "I want you to take the harder classes, Seth," she said. "I'm not

61

going to pretend otherwise. But you're not a little boy. You're the one who is going to have to do the studying. You've got to make up your own mind.''

"I've made up my mind,'' I said. "I want to take the easier classes.''

She nodded. "Sleep on it. If you feel the same way in the morning, I'll mail the schedule on my way to work.''

I took a shower and hit the sack. Around two o'clock in the morning I woke up sweating like a pig. I stumbled to the bathroom and sucked down some water. As I drank, I looked at myself in the mirror. That's when I knew I couldn't take the soft schedule.

It wasn't that I cared that much about going to a big-time college or being in the honors program. I was afraid that if I backed off on the schoolwork, I might start backing off on hard ground balls, I might start stepping in the bucket on inside fastballs. I was afraid if I didn't go all out in everything, I wouldn't go all out in anything. I'd go back to being the kind of guy I was before I met Jimmy. And I didn't want that. I didn't want that at all.

5♦

That season with the Redwood City Reds was tough. I wanted to make myself a better player, but there was nobody to talk to for advice.

Take bunting. I'd read in books that you had to get the bat head out front. But I didn't know what that meant. When I asked Coach Loffler, he stuck me in the batting cage and had me bunt ten times. He'd yell "Good bunt'' if the ball was fair or "You can do better!" if the ball dribbled foul. That was his idea of teaching. Eventually I figured out that getting the bat out in front means you've got to get your bat into fair territory and bunt the ball before it reaches home plate. But figuring things out on my own made for slow going.

It didn't help that our team was full of holes. We didn't have any speed, and without Jimmy, we didn't have a power RBI guy. Our first baseman had hands of stone, and our center fielder shied away from line drives.

As the losses piled up, I'd whine at home about what a terrible coach Loffler was. I suppose I was trying to make my mother feel bad about not letting me play on the Belmont Braves, though I don't know why. A couple of days after Jimmy's phone call, I'd seen Mr. Mongolin at Safeway. The second I saw him I found myself thinking that he was a cheater. And I knew right then and there that I didn't ever want anybody to look at me and think, "He is a cheater."

6♦

One game on our schedule was special — the game against the Belmont Braves. When it was a month away, I was looking forward to it the way you look forward to your birthday. When it was two weeks off, I felt a kind of nervousness creeping over me. The final week before the game I was almost sick.

Getting to see Jimmy again was a big deal for me, but what if it was no big deal for him? What if he saw me and nodded, and that was that? I didn't have any real friends on the Redwood City Reds, but that didn't mean Jimmy hadn't made new friends. Through him I'd learned everything I knew about baseball, but I hadn't taught him anything.

The day of the game I headed over to the park two hours early. I thought I'd be the first guy there, but Jimmy was already hitting balls off a tee into the batting cage. I stood off and watched him for five minutes or so.

His swing was sweet — I'd forgotten how sweet. But there was a crazy fury in him, too. That craziness had always been there, I guess, only now it was right there, right out front, instead of hiding.

I kept thinking he'd see me, but he never did. He ripped ball after ball into the batting cage, retrieved them, smacked them again. It was like he was trying to batter the ball into oblivion.

"Hey, Jimmy," I finally called out, "what's up?"

He jumped a little, but when he saw it was me, his face relaxed. "Seth, I was hoping you'd show up early. How's it going?"

"Okay. How about with you?"

He nodded. "Okay. You want to play a little catch?"

I've played catch a million times. But that time was special. It was just him and me, and a little wind, and the wet grass. As we tossed the ball back and forth, neither of us said a word, but it was like getting to know him again. The way he turned his shoulder in before he threw, the little flip of the glove he gave as he caught the ball — things like that were better than a lot of talk.

Pretty soon other guys started showing up. I tried tun-

64

ing them out, and I think Jimmy did, too. Finally his coach blew a whistle. "Belmont Braves over here."

There was no tuning that out. I threw the ball to Jimmy one final time. "Good luck," I said.

He laughed. "You're going to need the luck." Then he pulled a little grass out of the ground, tossed it in the air. "Watch out on the pop-ups, Seth. The wind is swirling today."

I nodded before heading to my teammates.

We started hot. A walk, an error, another walk to me, and a long double brought across three runs in the first. Our pitcher held Belmont scoreless the first two innings, even though Jimmy drove a triple to the base of the fence in his first at bat. Heading to the third, I thought we might pull off the upset.

But baseball can drive you crazy. A bloop hit — that's what did us in. A little broken-bat job that plopped onto the grass in left field barely two feet out of our third baseman's reach. That bloop hit came with two out in the third, and after that came everything. The Braves whistled base hits all over the park. Line shots down the right-field line. Long fly balls into the power alleys. Grounders through the hole. With five runs in, Jimmy unloaded a three-run homer to left.

Belmont scored four more in the fourth, three in the fifth. It was a laugher — for them. For us it was torture. The innings crawled by.

Jimmy was amazing, though. With his team way ahead, you'd think he'd let up a little, but he didn't. In the field, he kept his glove down in the dirt, his eyes on the batter, anticipating, always anticipating.

65

The score was 15–4 in the sixth when Jimmy banged out his fourth hit, a one-out single to right. As he led off first, I looked over at him. I couldn't yell out, "Way to go!" But I wanted to catch his eye, to give him a nod that meant the same thing.

That's why my head wasn't into the game, why I wasn't ready for the ground ball that came — a perfect two-hopper that should have resulted in an easy twin killing. I didn't charge the ball like I should have. And I double-clutched before I unloaded to Brad Comin, who was covering second.

I've relived the next moment a million times. I can still see Comin pivot; I can still see Jimmy barreling in on him. And I can still see Comin pinwheeling into the air. But most of all I remember Comin landing, and the weird way his knee bent under him, and the sound it made, a popping sound I've never heard before or since. Comin lay still, a glazed look on his face. Both coaches rushed out. "Somebody call nine-one-one," Loffler yelled.

Within minutes the Medic One came. One of the men gently moved Comin's lower leg. "Does that hurt?" he asked.

"No," Comin said, his face white. "I don't feel *anything.*"

As they lifted him onto the stretcher, his lower leg flopped like a strand of cooked spaghetti.

Jimmy was standing off by himself. I worked my way over to him. "Don't feel bad. It wasn't your fault."

He wheeled on me, and I felt those eyes again. "It was his own fault. He should have been off the bag."
66

The aid car roared off, siren wailing. The game was called. As I packed up my equipment bag, the guys on my team were cursing Jimmy, talking about what a dirty player he was. I didn't say anything to them, but I knew it wasn't that simple.

Coaches say you're supposed to give it your all every minute of every game. That's what Jimmy did, and it's stupid, and coaches shouldn't say it. With the score the way it was, Jimmy should have peeled off toward center field or slid so that his foot just reached the bag. If he'd done either of those things, Comin wouldn't have spent that summer on crutches.

But Jimmy wasn't the only one to blame. I should have been on my toes, playing the game, not back on my heels being a cheerleader for Jimmy. If I'd charged that ball and gotten my throw off cleanly, nothing would have happened.

And it was Comin's fault, too. We weren't little kids playing our first game. The second I double-clutched on the throw, Comin should have known he didn't have a prayer to turn a double play. Hc should have stepped on the bag, and gotten off as fast as he could. The throw to first did him in — and that throw was bad baseball.

I visited Comin in the hospital. He was down in the dumps. His knee was going to need an operation. He didn't know when he was getting out or how much physical therapy he was going to have to do. I hung around for half an hour or so, listening and not saying much, before heading for the door.

"Only one other guy has even visited me," Comin said before I made it.

"Who was that?" I asked.

"The guy who nailed me."

"Jimmy Winter?" I replied, amazed.

"Yeah, that's the guy. You know him?"

"Yeah, I know him. What did he say?"

Comin frowned. "Not much. He said he was sorry, but then he told me I shouldn't have been on the bag. He wasn't here two minutes."

I stared at Comin, lying there in that big, white bed. He didn't understand how hard it must have been for Jimmy to do what he'd done. And he wasn't in the mood to listen to me explain it to him. I guess if my leg looked like his, I wouldn't have wanted to hear it either.

"Hey, you'll come again, won't you?" Comin yelled out as I stepped into the hallway.

"Sure. I'll come again. You can count on it."

I meant to keep that promise. I planned to go back to the hospital, or visit Comin at home, but I never made it.

I've played a lot of baseball since then, in leagues and in pickup games at parks. In all that time I've never seen Comin play. I'd like to think he moved away or something. I hate thinking that he can't play, that his leg never got back to normal.

7♦

The first couple of weeks at Woodside High School were tough. I had trouble beating the tardy bell, trouble remembering what books to bring, trouble opening my locker. Even gym class was a pain. I never had enough time to shower, and some clown kept stealing my towel.

But once I got a couple of tests under my belt, and once I could get my locker open on the first try, Woodside didn't seem so impossible. The honors classes were hard, and I had more homework. But I did my assignments, and my grades didn't drop any. One week followed the next. The whole time I had my eye on spring and the beginning of baseball season.

As baseball season grew closer, the word got out that there would be a new coach of the freshman baseball team. One kid, whose mom worked in the office, said it was going to be a man who didn't even teach at Woodside.

That had some guys upset. "I wish they'd let us play varsity," Todd Franks, the best athlete in my gym class, said. "I hate the idea of wasting a year with some nobody."

I was jittery the day of baseball sign-ups. We were supposed to meet in the cafeteria at 3:15. It wasn't even 3:00 when I got there, and Franks was the only other person in the room. At 3:20 I counted sixteen guys total. I realized making the team would be no problem, and some of my nervousness went away.

At 3:30 the door opened. In walked the school secretary, Mrs. Holly. She passed out registration and insurance forms, gave us our practice and game schedules, that kind of stuff. I shoved the papers into my book bag.

"Your coach phoned," she said as she headed for the door. "He says he'll be here soon and to wait if you can."

69

"Who is he?" somebody called to her.

She shrugged. "A new guy. I can't remember his name."

We sat ten more minutes before the door burst open and a tall, burly man with a short red beard charged in. He was young, probably not even thirty. "My name is Rick Sharront," he said before the door closed behind him.

He talked so fast I couldn't follow. I know he said something about baseball being the only game that has a life of its own, whatever that means. And he said that every baseball — and I think he meant the ball itself — had a soul, and that no football had a soul, and no soccer ball or basketball or Ping-Pong ball had one either. The whole time he spoke his arms were waving, and he paced back and forth like a big dog stuck in a small cage. He stopped as suddenly as he'd started. "Our first practice is Tuesday. See you there." Then he was gone.

"What a geek!" somebody in the back blurted out, bringing laughter from around the room.

"Ah, give him a break," another kid answered.

I couldn't shake the feeling that I'd heard the name Rick Sharront before. I felt like I'd seen him, too, when he was younger, without the beard. But I couldn't figure out where. As I did my homework that night I kept trying to place him.

I was reading about the Roaring Twenties when it came to me. I opened my desk drawer and pulled out the baseball cards Jimmy had given me. There he was. Ricky Sharront — Cleveland Indians.

70

I flipped his card over. Four years in the minors, then eighteen games with the Indians, all at third base. Thirty-eight at bats, nine hits, three RBIs, three runs scored, one double, no triples, one home run.

I stared at the card for a long time. So what if he was strange, I thought. The man had hit a ball out of the park in the major leagues. Millions of guys play baseball; not many ever do that.

In the locker room before our first practice, I told my teammates. "He's too weird to have been in the majors," Todd Franks said. "It must be some other Rick Sharront."

"Ask him," I answered. "He'll tell you."

"You ask him," Franks returned.

Before practice started, Sharront had us sit down on the infield grass facing him. "Boys," he said, arms waving again, "as far as I'm concerned, there's nothing better you can do with your time than to play baseball. So I'm not much on picky rules. I don't care what clothes you wear, how long your hair is, whether you pierce your ears or pluck your eyebrows. I want you here — on the baseball diamond — not out drinking or getting your girlfriend pregnant.

"But that doesn't mean I don't have rules. In baseball you get three strikes before you're out. And that's how I run my program.

"I'm not going to try to run down every thing that could be counted against you. You know what I mean. Big stuff. Failing classes, alcohol, drugs, theft. The first time, you're suspended a game. The second time, two games. But if there's a third time — and I hope to God this never comes up — but if there is a third time, then I'm going to have to figure you're the bad apple and I'm going to heave you out of the barrel." He paused. "I've had my say. Any of you have anything you want cleared up?"

A couple of guys looked over at me.

"Ask him," one of them whispered.

I raised my hand. "Did you play for the Cleveland Indians?"

I figured he'd be happy somebody knew, that he'd puff and brag a little. But it was the opposite. His body sagged, like he'd been punched in the stomach.

"Yeah, I played," he said. He tugged at his beard for a second. "Do you know what it means when they say a player has a cup of coffee in the majors?"

He was looking straight at me.

"It means a guy makes the majors, but doesn't stick."

"Well, I had a sip of a cup of coffee."

Everything went quiet for a minute. Sharront blew his whistle. "Okay, let's get started."

After we stretched, Sharront told us he wanted to check our speed. I figured he'd have us run the fifty-yard dash, but instead he put us at home plate, had us hit a ball, and then timed how long it took us to make it to first base. Then he had us work on getting out of the box quicker.

After we'd sweated out a couple of hours of drills, Sharront called us to him. "That was great! Super practice! We'll do a lot more of that. Fundamentals — that's the name of the game. Right now you're young men who play baseball. I'm going to turn you into baseball play-
72

ers." He paused. "Let's run two miles and call it a day."

We thought he was joking. We'd done nothing but run for two hours. But Sharront headed for the track, so we trudged behind him. He lined us up, blew his whistle, and we took off.

A strange thing happened then. Most coaches are real good at blowing their whistles and telling you to run while they scratch their fat bellies. But Sharront didn't stand — he ran with us.

Actually, he ran ahead of us. Junior Tupo kept up with him for the first mile, but at the finish Sharront had him by fifty yards easy.

I finished in the middle of the pack. My side ached; my face was bright red; my throat was filled with snotty spit. I leaned forward, gasping for air. Sharront patted me on the back. "Nice run, kid. Nice run." He wasn't even winded.

When I finally had the strength to look up, Todd Franks was crossing the finish line, last by two hundred yards. He'd barely broken a sweat. "Was that your best effort?" Sharront barked at him.

"I never was good at track," Franks replied coolly.

8♦

The next afternoon Sharront broke us into groups by position. Infielders here, catchers there, pitchers some place else. I don't know how he did it, but it seemed like he was everywhere at once, giving advice, shouting instructions, waving his arms around.

Sharront hadn't lied; he was a maniac for fundamentals. According to him, none of us knew how to throw, how to catch, how to slide, how to swing a bat. "Not that way," he'd say. "Like this." Then he'd clap his hands together and scream, "Keep trying! Keep trying!" He screamed all the time, but he wasn't one of the hardnosed drill sergeant types. When Sharront yelled, it was a happy yell — if that makes sense.

Most of us busted our tails running the bases, hitting the cutoff man, backing up throws, laying down bunts, taking infield, fielding pop-ups, working pick-off plays and rotation plays. "All the little things," Sharront kept telling us, "add up to big things. You've got to buy in to my system if we're going to win."

But not everybody bought in. According to Todd Franks, everything about Sharront was stupid. The way he ran practice, the clothes he wore, the way he clapped his hands. Everything.

It's bad to have any player ridiculing the coach. But when it's the guy on your team who hits the ball the farthest and runs the fastest, that's real trouble. It didn't take long before Todd had some followers. Not many; maybe three or four guys. But those guys dogged it every time Sharront wasn't watching them. And they dogged the two-mile run at the end of practice. That made the rest of us feel stupid for working so hard.

The final practice before our opener was strictly on defense. Sharront stood at the plate, bat and ball in hand. He'd yell out a situation. "First and third, nobody out, second inning, tie game." Then he'd bang the ball at one of the fielders. If the fielder went to the right base,

74

he'd quiz the rest of us on why it was right. If he went to the wrong base, Sharront would quiz him. That's all we did, over and over. At the end, Sharront dragged us to the track and whipped us all in the two-mile run — as usual.

"That was the dumbest of the whole bunch of dumb practices," Franks griped in the shower room. He went on and on, calling Sharront a two-bit bush leaguer, a loser.

I was boiling. I wished Jimmy were there. Jimmy would have told Franks to keep his fat mouth shut. And Franks would have, too, if Jimmy said it.

9♦

We opened at home against Menlo Atherton. I checked the lineup card as I entered the locker room. I was starting at second base, which was great, but Sharront had me batting eighth. That I didn't like at all.

It's funny how things work. Before the season started, I thought that making the freshman team was all I wanted. After I'd made the team, I thought if I could start at second base, I wouldn't care where I hit in the order. But seeing my name in the eight spot made me burn inside. Right then and there I vowed to get some hits, to push my way up the batting order.

Once we were in uniform, Sharront called us together. "We're going to pressure these guys. We're going to hit-and-run, bunt, steal bases, squeeze runners home. On defense hit the cutoff man, throw to the right base, make the plays. Now let's go get them!''

That's when the butterflies hit. I don't even remember throwing the ball around before the game. But I do remember the ump yelling "Play ball!'' And I remember crouching, looking in at the batter, waiting for the first pitch in my first game of high-school baseball.

Our pitcher, John Kister, wound and came in with a fastball across the heart of the plate. Strike one.

The season was under way.

I caught a quick break. Their leadoff hitter bounced a two-hopper to me. I fielded, straightened up, and threw him out. Making that first play killed some of those butterflies.

Todd Franks led off our half of the second inning with a triple. With one out, he scored on a single to right. I came to the plate with two gone and a runner at first.

Before stepping into the box, I looked down at Sharront coaching at third base. Sharront did a zillion things with his hands, but that was to confuse Menlo Atherton. I watched his feet. Before I stepped back in the box, he scratched the dirt with his right toe: hit-and-run.

I could feel the sweat come to my palms. The runner would take off on the pitch. The second baseman would cover the bag, leaving a hole between first and second. My job was to punch the ball into that hole.

Their pitcher came in with a curve on the outside corner of the plate. I swung down and through, hitting a ground ball that took three hops and skittered into right field. The lead runner made it to third without a throw. Sharront clapped and gave me the thumbs-up sign.

76

Our number-nine batter, Sean Taylor, wasn't much at the plate. So we'd need some luck to score the second run. But having a runner on third puts the screws on the other team. The catcher can't afford a passed ball, and since most catchers have trouble controlling a curveball, the hitter can figure he's going to see nothing but fastballs. That's what Sharront told us, anyway.

But knowing a fastball is coming doesn't mean you can hit it. Taylor's first swing was an hour late. On the next pitch, Sharront put the steal on for me — a gutsy call. I've got average speed, so a good throw is going to nail me and end the inning.

Their pitcher stretched, looked over. On his motion toward the plate I took off. Maybe seeing me leave spooked him, because his pitch was down in the dirt and skipped all the way to the backstop. The run scored, and I ended up at third. "Way to execute," Sharront said, and he patted me on the back.

Taylor struck out to strand me, but the whole team felt good as we headed out for the third. We'd put the pressure on Menlo Atherton, and they'd crumpled like Sharront said they would. I looked at Franks as we ran out to the field. "Not bad for a geek coach," I wanted to yell, but I didn't have the guts.

After your team scores, it's important to keep the other team from scoring in their next at bat. If you keep them down, they usually stay down. But if they score, they start thinking they can come back.

So it wasn't good when their leadoff hitter banged a single right up the middle. Kister struck out the next hitter, and the guy after that grounded to short. Our shortstop, Bob Ward, made an okay play on the ball, and we got the force-out, but there was no way I could turn two. As I went back to my position, I couldn't help thinking that if Jimmy were at shortstop, we would have gotten the double play to end the inning.

Still, a guy on first with two outs isn't exactly a rally. But then Kister walked the next two guys, loading up the bases. Sharront was going crazy, pacing around and waving his arms. "Throw strikes!" he kept yelling. "Throw strikes!"

Sure enough, Kister did throw a strike to the next hitter. Only it was right down the middle with nothing on it. Menlo Atherton's hitter laced it to the fence in left center, driving in three runs.

That's okay, I thought. *We're down one run, but one run is no big deal.* But their next hitter singled. Then came a double, a home run, another double, a walk, a double. Sharront took Kister out, brought in Cary Barstow. Bang — a single. Finally . . . finally, a strikeout to end the inning. Nine to two, Menlo Atherton.

In baseball, when you're way behind you can't take chances. You can't steal, you can't hit-and-run, you can't try for the extra base. All the things we practiced, all the things that Sharront wanted to be the signature of our team — all of them were useless. To make things worse, Menlo Atherton kept shellacking the ball. By the time the game ended, they'd scored sixteen runs.

In the locker room after it was over, Sharront told us to hold our heads high. "Blowouts happen. Don't get discouraged."

I felt basically okay walking home — as okay as you

78

can feel when you lose by thirteen runs.

At Massachusetts Avenue a black Thunderbird came flying around the corner, wheels squealing. It must have been the noise that frightened the cocker spaniel. The dog raced right into the street, barking. The driver swerved — I'll give him that — but he still hit the dog. The spaniel was thrown fifteen, twenty feet in the air. The driver slammed on his brakes. The passenger door opened; a girl's face peered out for an instant. Then the door slammed shut and the driver burned rubber as he tore away.

Some things you just know. As I ran over to that dog, I knew he didn't have a chance. He was lying on his side, panting heavily, blood trickling from his mouth. I kneeled down, took his head into my hands, looked into his eyes. I could see fear. "You're going to be okay," I whispered. He blinked a few times, closed his eyes, opened them once more. Then the breath went out of him for the final time. The whole thing was over in a minute.

From behind me I heard a little girl. "Boss!" she screamed, and she burst into tears. I stepped aside and watched as she knelt next to her dog. Behind her were her parents, and then the neighbors crowded around. "Did anybody see what happened?" the girl's father called out.

He asked me some questions, but I hadn't gotten a license number or even seen the driver. The girl's father shook his head. "Some drunk high-school kid." He covered the dog with his jacket; then he led his daughter, still sobbing, back into their house.

I stood a little longer, looking at the shape underneath the jacket, thinking that it wasn't fair, that nothing should ever have to die, ever. But I also felt strangely glad that I had been there, glad that I had been able to comfort the cocker spaniel at the final moment.

The entire walk home I found myself thinking about my father, about his last moments. I wished that someone, even a stranger, had been with him when he died.

I didn't tell my mother what happened. I don't know why; I just didn't. And I thought I acted normally that night. But before my mother went to bed, she twice asked if something was wrong. Both times I told her I was fine, but I know she didn't believe me. Sometimes I can *feel* my mother thinking about my father. I guess she can feel it when I'm thinking about him.

10♦

We lost our next game, and the game after that, and five games more after that. We were down but Sharront wasn't. At practice he was always upbeat, always harping on his precious fundamentals.

The man was a perfectionist. He'd go over something again and again until everybody had it right. And as a reward for getting it right, he'd blow his whistle and scream, "All right, gentlemen, let's run our two miles."

We played well in the first couple of games we lost. Only a couple of errors, no stupid plays. Almost everybody hustled. We might have held together if it hadn't been for Franks.

In the stat book Franks was the only guy on our team

having a great year. He had four home runs, sixteen RBIs, and was batting over .400. But he was dogging every drill at practice and raking Sharront in the shower room afterward. And with every loss, another guy would start acting like him.

By the fourth game, players started missing signs, throwing to the wrong bases, not backing up plays. The little things — the things that Sharront had us work on so hard — those were the things we stopped doing.

An outsider wouldn't have noticed any change. But Sharront noticed. "Every day you guys give me less," he'd say. "We'll never win till you start giving more."

At practice after our eighth loss, Franks ditched a sliding drill by claiming to have dirt in his eye, and then tried to skip the two-mile run at the end of practice. "I twisted my ankle," he told Sharront.

Sharront wasn't a fool. "Franks, I'm not going to make you run if you say you're injured. But I am going to make you look me straight in the eye and say it again."

Franks stared right at him. "My ankle hurts."

Sharront turned his head and spit. "You're excused."

The following game against St. Francis was typical. Devon Maxwell, our leadoff hitter, walked. I was batting second that game, and I laid down a sacrifice bunt to move him up. Junior Tupo followed with a pop-up to third. That put it on Todd Franks's shoulders, and he came through. He took a change-up out of the park to straightaway center. He absolutely crushed it. We were up 2–0, and the sight of that ball leaving the park had gotten the adrenaline flowing.

81

But the thing about losing is that you start to expect things to go wrong, and when you expect bad things to happen, they do. By the bottom of the fifth, we'd committed three errors; our pitchers had given up six hits and walked four. Franks laced an RBI single in the fourth, but we were still behind, 7–3.

Then something strange happened. We rallied. Maxwell looped a double down the right-field line to lead off the sixth. I worked a walk. Tupo took a ferocious swing and hit a squibber up the third-base line. By the time St. Francis's pitcher fielded the ball, everybody was safe. That brought Todd Franks to the plate with the bases loaded and nobody out.

Their pitcher came in with a fastball, and Franks was sitting on it. He sent a rocket screaming into left center. I held up in between second and third until I saw the ball bounce, then I took off and scored standing, with Tupo right behind me. Sharront was holding up his hands to stop Franks at third, but he ran right through the sign. He wanted that grand slam.

The shortstop cut off the throw from the outfield, wheeled, and fired a perfect strike to the plate. Instead of sliding, Franks put his shoulder down and barreled into the catcher. When the dust settled, the catcher was rolling around in the dirt holding his shoulder and moaning, and the ball was lying on the ground in front of the plate. "Safe!" screamed the umpire, and our whole team came unglued. We didn't score any more runs that inning, but we were pumped as we picked up our gloves and headed for the field.

"Sit down, Franks," Sharront said quietly as he came

in from the third-base coach's box. "You've done enough damage for one day. Matt Lester's taking your spot in center."

"What?" Franks said, astonished. "Why am I coming out?"

"Think about it," Sharront replied. "And if you can't figure it out, think some more."

We ended up losing 9–7. In our last at bat, Lester struck out looking with runners at first and third.

After the game Franks confronted Sharront.

"I scored, didn't I? I was safe."

"Doesn't matter."

"What do you mean it doesn't matter! I hit a grand slam and you say it doesn't matter!" Franks was screaming.

"I mean it doesn't matter. You run through my signs, and you'll sit."

"You can't bench me. I'm the best player you've got."

Sharront laughed. "We've lost every game with you. We can't do any worse without you."

Franks slammed his glove down. "I don't need this. I quit."

Sharront didn't blink. "Have your uniform laundered before you turn it in. Otherwise there's a ten-dollar fee."

11♦

As I dragged myself home that day, my mind was a jumble. Franks had gotten what he deserved. I knew that. Still, you can't lose your best player and not pay a price. My stomach turned when I thought about the seven games left to play.

I felt so low I didn't look up as I opened the front door. That's why I heard his voice before I saw him.

"Hey, Seth, what's going on?"

Sitting on the sofa was Jimmy Winter.

My mother brought out two bowls of ice cream and then left us alone. I guess she figured we'd have a lot to talk about. And I suppose we did, but for a long time we couldn't connect. It was like I knew him, but didn't know him; like he was both my best friend and a total stranger.

"My mom and I are back in the old house," Jimmy said. "Starting tomorrow I'll be going to Woodside too."

I wanted to ask if the divorce was off, but I couldn't get the words out. We talked about nothing for a while. Then he said he had to go.

"I'll walk partway with you," I said.

The sky was black; no moon, no stars even. Walking a couple of blocks in that blackness made it easier to talk.

"How's your father doing?" I asked, almost in a whisper.

Jimmy looked down. "He shows up once in a while, but I don't see him much."

"And your mom?"

He shrugged. "She's better, I guess. We're moving back, so she's not so afraid anymore. Her big thing is still for my father to get counseling. She thinks that if he stopped drinking they could get back together."

"Maybe they could."

Jimmy scoffed at the idea. "He'll never change. Besides, he's got his girlfriend." He paused, and when he spoke again his voice was hard. "You know what I wish, Seth? I wish he would move away, to Alaska or New York or somewhere. I wish I never had to see him again for as long as I live."

"You don't mean that," I said.

"Yes I do," Jimmy said with conviction. "Yes I do."

12◆

I knew Jimmy wasn't in the honors program, but I hoped he'd be in my gym class or my French class. It turned out he wasn't taking a foreign language, and he had gym first period while I had it third. So the only time we had together was lunch.

In the cafeteria I plunked my tray down next to his. I started to ask how his classes had gone, but he wanted to talk baseball. "Why didn't you tell me your coach was Rick Sharront?"

"I don't know," I said. "I didn't think about it."

"You didn't think about it! You've got a major leaguer as a coach and you didn't think about it!"

I tried to explain. "This season hasn't worked out — not for him and not for us." I rattled on about our losing streak, and about Todd Franks quitting.

Jimmy was silent for a long time when I finished. I knew he was thinking about something. Then, just before lunch ended, he came out with it. "I know the season is almost over, but do you think I might still be able

85

to get on the team? I mean, since this Franks guy quit."

"I don't know," I said, excited at the idea. "But it can't hurt to ask."

That afternoon Sharront ran Jimmy through a quick tryout while the rest of us warmed up. Jimmy fielded grounders for about five minutes; then Sharront called him in for batting practice. Kister pitched, and Jimmy smacked four of the first dozen pitches he saw out of the park.

His swing looked perfect to me — but not to Sharront. He took the bat out of Jimmy's hands and started demonstrating changes he wanted. "You're overstriding, and you're opening up your left shoulder too soon. You don't want to become a dead pull hitter. You'll get a few more home runs, but you'll lose thirty points off your batting average." Sharront handed the bat back to Jimmy. "Try it my way."

If I'd been Jimmy, I'd have been burned. He'd pounded the cover off the ball. What more did Sharront want?

But Jimmy wasn't me. He took the bat back, and for the next dozen pitches he tried to do exactly what Sharront wanted, even though all it got him were a bunch of dribblers and pop-ups.

"Stick with it," Sharront said when they finished. "Those changes will pay off for you. Now let's go to my office."

When Jimmy came out, he was carrying Todd Franks's uniform over his arm.

* * *

I hadn't given up on the season. None of the guys had. Or at least we didn't think we had. But at 0-9, we didn't have quite the same zip we had on the first day of practice. That's why Jimmy made us look bad.

He played like he always did — all out. He took grounders off his chest; he slid hard into the bases; he backed up every play. At the plate he swung only at strikes in his zone. "That's how you should all be playing!" Sharront yelled. "Like Jimmy Winter. He has been here only one day and he already understands what I want."

A player like that can become pretty unpopular pretty fast. "Tell your red-hot buddy to cool it tomorrow," Junior Tupo muttered to me as we headed over to the track once practice had ended. Sharront lined us up, blew his whistle, and we took off.

I should have known Jimmy wouldn't fall back into the pack and let Sharront run away from him. Jimmy never let anybody beat him in anything without a fight. But I didn't think Jimmy had a real chance to win.

Sharront held the lead the first mile, but Jimmy stayed within four or five strides. Between a mile and a mile and a half, Jimmy faded. He dropped eight strides back . . . ten . . . twelve.

I figured it was over, but with half a mile to go, Jimmy picked it up. He didn't sprint. Nobody sprints an 880. He pumped his legs a tiny bit faster, and with every stride he cut into Sharront's lead.

I was running with four or five other guys. We were maybe sixty yards behind. Our eyes were glued on Jimmy. It was like he was running for all of us.

With one lap to go, Jimmy pulled even. Sharront looked over, then kicked a little. He pulled five yards ahead, then ten. With 220 left, Sharront was at least fifteen yards in front, but you could see he was feeling it.

I kept hoping Jimmy would reel him in with a little sprint of his own, but it didn't look like he had anything left. Sharront was laboring, no doubt about it, but from the 220 mark to the 100-yard mark, he held his lead.

That's when Jimmy put the pedal to the floor. It's not many times that you think of human beings as animals, but that's what it was: one animal chasing down another one. Jimmy's arms pumped; his legs drove into the cinder track; he sucked air by the gallon.

With about sixty-five yards left Sharront completely tied up. That's the worst feeling in the world. Everybody who runs knows it. Your legs feel like redwood trees. You gasp for air, and you can't get enough. Your lungs burn, and there's a knife in your guts. Track guys call it having a bear on your back, but to me it feels more like a mountain.

Jimmy caught Sharront with thirty yards to go, and he roared by him like a train roars by a station without riders. Sharront staggered in, then collapsed on the infield grass, his face bright red.

I crossed the finish line about thirty seconds later. Instead of feeling dead exhausted, I was exhilarated, and so were the rest of the guys. We gathered around Jimmy, patting him on the back and giving him a good shake. He looked like he might puke. We didn't care. If we'd had the energy, we would have picked him up and carried him to the shower room.

I don't think I knew how much Sharront's victories were eating at me until Jimmy put an end to them. It was as if we were all living in someone's shadow. Jimmy brought us out into the light.

13♦

The next practice Jimmy was the leader of the team. Instead of looking at him like he was some weird gung ho type, the other guys copied his hustle. A fire was in our practice that hadn't been there before. The smile on Sharront's face went ear-to-ear, and it stayed there even when Jimmy whipped him again in the two-mile run. Then, right before our next game, Sharront announced that Jimmy would be batting third and starting at shortstop.

It's amazing when you think about it. A guy joins at the tail end of the season, and within a week he's the heart of the team. But nobody griped. Jimmy had earned it.

The game was on Saturday morning, ten o'clock. We took a little batting practice, tossed the ball around the infield. The umpire looked at his clock and yelled, "Play ball!" I settled into my spot between first and second, crouched, and waited for Kister to deliver the first pitch.

That's when Jimmy started. "Hey batter batter!" he screamed as the Bellarmine leadoff batter came to the plate. None of us had ever gotten into any chatter, not even during our early games. But Jimmy was screaming on every pitch. "Humm Baby, Humm Baby, Humm."

Jimmy yelled all by himself for the first half-dozen pitches of the game. Dan Hill, our third baseman, looked over at me. *How can it hurt?* I thought. So I started. "Easy out! Easy out!" I chirped. Once I started, Hill took it up. "Heyyyyyyyyy — Swing!" It was stupid, but it was fun. And we hadn't had much fun that year.

Bellarmine went down in order.

Their pitcher started the game wild, walking our lead-off hitter, Devon Maxwell, and then plunking me with a slow curve. That brought Jimmy up with a chance to knock in a run and maybe start a big inning.

That first at bat is tough, no matter what league you are in, no matter how good you are. Your heart is pounding, and you're fighting your nerves as much as the pitcher.

Jimmy took a fastball outside. The Bellarmine pitcher went into his stretch, delivered. Jimmy took that velvet-smooth swing and caught the ball on the sweet spot. The ball rocketed off his bat. Their center fielder ran about five steps back, stopped, looked up. Jimmy's home run cleared the center-field fence by fifty feet.

The guys were so stunned they hardly clapped. Even Sharront was speechless. In the Bellarmine dugout players were pointing to where the ball had landed and were shaking their heads.

When Jimmy started with the chatter in the second inning, we all took it up, infielders and outfielders, without even thinking about it. "You're a bum . . . You're no good . . . You swing like an old lady." The old, corny phrases filled the park.

We were into the game.

Bellarmine did zip for the next three innings. But we couldn't add to our lead. In the fifth they scratched out a run, and they scored again in the sixth on a two-out triple. Jimmy was still loose, still chattering, but the rest of us tightened. The apple was in our throats. We could feel another late-inning choke coming.

In the bottom of the sixth I laced a single into left, and when their left fielder bobbled it, I took off for second. I slid into the bag headfirst. It was a bang-bang play, but my hand caught the sack just before the glove slapped my wrist. The ump stretched his arms out. "Safe!"

It didn't look like my hustle would matter, though. Jimmy lined out; Junior Tupo popped up. But on a 2-2 pitch Hill blooped a single to right. I was off on contact and scored without a throw, putting us up 4–2.

Bellarmine was down to their last three outs. But Kister was tired. If we'd had a decent relief pitcher, Sharront would have brought him in.

Their first batter hit a scorcher right at Jimmy. It took a wicked bounce and caught him on the throat. He collapsed in a heap as the ball trickled into short left field. I raced over to Jimmy, and the Bellarmine player — seeing second base uncovered — cruised into second.

Jimmy was up by the time Sharront reached him. "I'm okay," he insisted. "It didn't catch me square." That took guts because the ball had caught Jimmy flush on the Adam's apple.

Bellarmine's next hitter popped up to first, but Kister walked the guy after that. The next batter roped Kister's first pitch into left to drive in a run, making the score 4–3, and putting runners at first and second with only one out.

I looked at Jimmy. His face had turned ghostly white, his eyes were glassy, and his lips were blue. He had to come out of the game.

But before I could call time, Kister stretched and delivered. The Bellarmine hitter ripped a shot between me and the first baseman. I got a good jump on the ball, and when I snagged it I was thinking double play. I wheeled and fired the ball to Jimmy. The Bellarmine base runner was barreling down on him, but Jimmy hung in there. He took the throw, dragged his foot across the bag, and blazed a strike to first just before he was creamed by a rolling slide. Jimmy's throw was in time. Double play . . . Game over . . . 4–3 Woodside!

We didn't celebrate, at least not right away, because Jimmy was lying on the ground, his head rocking back and forth like he had malaria. A doctor came out of the stands and told Jimmy to breathe nice and easy. Slowly he came back.

"Did we win?" were the first words out of his mouth.

14♦

The monkey was off our back and it stayed off. We won our next three games, 8–6, 6–5, and 7–6.

I'm usually a shower person, but my muscles ached

so much during that winning streak that after every practice, after every game, I'd slide into the tub and soak. The hot water would sting in a dozen places where my skin was raw.

The raw skin was why we were winning. Before Jimmy joined the team, I would have been insulted if somebody had told me I wasn't giving 100 percent. But I hadn't been. Those bruises proved it. Jimmy had that knack — he made me dig a little deeper inside, find a little more than I thought I had. And it wasn't just me. It was every guy on the team. Jimmy had the heart of a champion, and he pumped a little of his blood into our veins.

I was so caught up in our winning streak that I pretty much forgot about his father and all that. Maybe I didn't really forget; maybe it was more that I hoped the whole problem would go away.

But after practice one Thursday, as we were walking home along the Alameda, a car pulled up. "Hey, Jimmy. Hey, Seth. You boys want a ride?"

Mr. Winter was smiling broadly. Next to him was a new woman, even younger than his other girlfriend.

Jimmy turned bright red. Instead of answering, he stared first at his father, then at the woman, and finally at me. "That's okay, Mr. Winter," I said. "We just finished practice. The walk cools us down."

Mr. Winter kept smiling, but I could see the disappointment in his eyes. "Okay. Suit yourselves. It's good seeing you two. Maybe I'll catch a game sometime. Good-bye, Jimmy. Good-bye, Seth."

Jimmy still didn't answer.

93

"Good-bye, Mr. Winter," I managed for both of us.
We were quiet until we reached the corner where
Jimmy turned off. But just before he went his way, he
spoke, almost in a whisper. "Seth, sometimes I think
you're lucky your father is dead. At least you know
where you stand. I never know."

It was a strange thing to say, and if anybody else had
said it, I would have been angry. But coming from
Jimmy I understood. I suppose in a small way he was
right. I never really knew my father, so he didn't tear
me up day in and day out the way Jimmy's father tore
him up.

But Jimmy was wrong, too, wrong in a way he'd
never know. My father's death had left a hole in my life,
a hole that could never be filled. No matter what Jimmy's
father did, no matter how badly he acted, he was
there.

For me it's different. You can't see emptiness, but that
doesn't mean you don't feel it. I'm not saying I feel it
all the time. Days, even weeks go by and I don't think
of my father once. But then, out of the blue, the emptiness
comes.

15♦

After our fourth straight win, Todd Franks
pulled up a chair next to me while I was studying in the
library. "I hear you won again. That Jimmy Winter must
be some ballplayer."

"He's good," I said. "Real good."

Franks opened an atlas, but he wasn't in the library to

study. He wanted something. "Have you heard that Knecht won't coach varsity baseball next year, that he's retiring?"

"No."

"Well, he is. Word is that Sharront will take his place."

"Really?" I answered.

"It makes sense, doesn't it?" Franks went on. "You don't bring in a major leaguer to coach freshmen."

I nodded. "Yeah, I guess it does make sense."

"Seth, you know how Sharront thinks. Would he take me back on the team if I apologized?"

"I don't know. He might."

Franks stood. "I'm going to give it a try." He rapped his knuckles on the table. "I miss baseball. I didn't think I would, but I do."

It's hard to explain how I felt. Franks was a great player. With him and Jimmy, we'd be dynamite. Still, part of me hoped Sharront wouldn't let him back.

Sharront gave us the news before practice. "Todd Franks has rejoined the team. He's in the locker room dressing right now. I hope you're glad to have him back. I know I am."

I couldn't help watching Franks that afternoon. I guess we all did. It had been his team; he'd been our big stick. But now it was Jimmy's.

A run-in had to happen — and it came during the second hour of practice. While Sharront was working with the pitchers, Dan Hill was hitting balls to the rest of us.

Hill blooped a little pop into short center. Jimmy was

95

off with the crack of the bat. He ran out from under his cap, dived, and came up six inches short. He pulled himself to his feet and retrieved the ball. Then he glared out at Todd. "That was your ball!" he screamed.

Todd had jogged in; he hadn't even tried for the pop fly. Jimmy's anger took him by surprise. "This is practice, champ," he said. "Not the World Series."

Jimmy fixed Todd with those icy green eyes of his. "Don't call me 'champ.' And don't loaf. Nobody loafs on this team."

Todd's eyes narrowed. For an instant I thought the two of them would have it out right there. But a strange thing happened. Todd's face relaxed. "Sorry, Winter," he said. "It won't happen again." Then he trotted back to center field. On the next fly ball to center, Todd ran like it was the World Series.

With Franks playing hard, we were really something. We destroyed Carlmont, 11–3, and Palo Alto, 15–2. They had to stop the Palo Alto game after five innings because of darkness. Every starter had a hit; Jimmy and Todd both had four.

Our last game was against St. Francis. They'd clinched first place; we were in fifth place. If we lost, our season would be over. But if we won, at 7-9 we'd finish in fourth place and sneak into the playoffs. It was crazy, but that's how it worked. And once we were in, I figured we had a decent chance to take the title.

I wouldn't have said it out loud, but I thought we'd roll right over St. Francis. Even when they scored twice in the top of the first on a walk, an error, and a double, I didn't sweat it. I don't think the other guys did either.

I figured we'd pound out as many hits and as many runs as we needed. Winning streaks make you feel that way. As I went to the bat rack in the bottom of the first, Jimmy slid up next to me. "Recognize the pitcher?" he asked. I looked out toward the mound. The guy looked familiar, but I couldn't place him. "Listen to the catcher's glove pop. That's Steve Cannon. I'm sure of it."

My mouth dropped open. I took one deep breath, then another, and another. I was trying to slow my heartbeat. If I was going to hit Cannon, I couldn't be afraid of him.

I didn't even watch Devon Maxwell's at bat. I swung two bats in the on-deck circle and told myself over and over that Cannon was just another pitcher. Then I heard the umpire yell, "Strike three!"

I wasn't beaten before I went up there. I really wasn't. I told myself I could hit Cannon, and I thought I could. Until the first pitch. Then it was as if I were back in Little League again. Cannon's first fastball blew by me like an express train. He reared back and fired another one, and then one more, and I sat down.

I wasn't the only one. Cannon struck out almost everybody else, too. Jimmy got a double in the fourth, and Todd followed with an RBI single. But that was our only run. Cannon had spells of wildness when he'd walk a couple of guys. Still, he always had his fastball when he needed it.

St. Francis's 2–1 lead held all the way to our last at bats. As we came in, gloom settled over us. Three more outs and we wouldn't make the playoffs.

Jimmy took a bat and raked it against the fence, trying to wake us up. "Give me a chance, guys!" he screamed.

97

"Give me one more at bat. I can hit this guy."

I knew he could. We all knew he could. He was magic. If we could get him to the plate, he'd do it for us. But that was a big if. He was hitting sixth in the inning.

Cannon started off like it would be over in nine pitches. He threw three blazing strikes right past our first guy. But our pinch hitter, Keith May, got lucky. He took a weak swing at an inside fastball. The ball dribbled up the first-base line — a swinging bunt he beat out easily.

We had some life. And Cannon was showing signs of tiring. His first pitch to Fred Pacheco was a slow curve way inside that caught Fred in the leg. Now we really did have something cooking. First and second, one out, Maxwell up.

St. Francis's coach walked slowly out to the mound. As I swung a bat in the on-deck circle, I was praying that he'd yank Cannon. The coach looked down to the bullpen a couple of times. Once he almost motioned, but he left Cannon in.

Maxwell didn't see any slow curveballs, that's for sure. Cannon reached back and whaled the ball. The first two pitches were strikes, but Cannon overthrew his third pitch, trying too hard. The ball sailed over the catcher's head. Both runners moved up a base. A single — a measly little base hit anywhere — and we'd win.

Maxwell tugged on the bill of his cap. Cannon stared in, wound, delivered. Maxwell spun away. "Strike three!" the ump yelled.

From the third-base coach's box, Sharront yelled at

the umpire. "What kind of call is that? The pitch almost hit him!"

The ump stepped in front of the plate, dusted it off. "Your boy bailed out," he snarled at Sharront, and then he motioned me into the batter's box.

I didn't have to win the game, but I had to keep the inning going. A walk, a hit-by-a-pitch — anything to get Jimmy to the plate.

I pulled the bat back, took a deep breath. Cannon delivered. A fastball, right down the pike. I saw it good, uncoiled as fast as I could, and fouled it straight back into the screen. I can't explain how wonderful that felt. It was just a crummy foul ball, but it meant that Cannon was tiring, that I had a chance.

I stepped out, tugged at my pants, stepped back in. Immediately Cannon went into his windup. A fastball — what else. Again I took a rip at it. This time I caught it solid, right in the sweet spot, but late. The ball shot down the right-field line, foul by twenty feet.

He glared at me. He stood on the mound and glared at me like a boxer glares at his opponent before a fight. I think he was insulted that I'd gotten my bat on the ball. But he didn't scare me. All he did was pump me up even more.

He went into his windup and delivered. The instant I picked the ball up, I pulled the trigger. And I was on it; I was on it perfectly.

Only it wasn't a fastball. Cannon had pulled the string, thrown me a change-up. I was way out in front. I tried to yank the bat back, but I couldn't. I was so off balance

99

I fell down as the ump yelled, "Strike three!" I felt like an idiot lying there in the dirt.

Jimmy grabbed me by the elbow and pulled me up. "Don't sweat it, Seth. You got your cuts. Besides, Cannon is the one who backed down."

16♦

In the locker room after the game, Todd invited Jimmy and me to a party at his house that Saturday. "I don't know," Jimmy said. "I'm not much for parties."

Todd looked disgusted. "Listen, Jimmy. I've done things your way, haven't I? Now the season's over. Time to try things my way. Okay?"

Jimmy laughed. "Okay."

Saturday night Jimmy and I caught a bus up the Alameda to Atherton. Todd had drawn us a map, but it was still hard to find his house. Atherton is real ritzy, and all the streets wind around.

When we finally found the number, we thought we had the wrong night or something. No music, hardly any lights — the big house looked deserted. Jimmy knocked on the door; we waited; he knocked again.

"There's no party," I said. "Let's get out of here."

Just then Todd's father opened the front door. He had jet black hair and was wearing a coat and tie. He introduced himself, asked us how we were doing, and then pointed to a path that led around back. "Todd's room is around there," he said. "Follow the walkway."

Todd's room turned out to be more like a small house. He had a bedroom, and then next to it a rec room with a pool table and refrigerator and a sink and a big-screen TV and an unbelievable stereo system.

Two other guys were there, Devon Maxwell and Junior Tupo. Both of them were drinking beer. "You guys want a brew?" Todd asked, opening up the refrigerator.

"No," Jimmy said. I shook my head, too.

We shot pool for a while, and watched the Giants play the Mets on the tube. Todd kept asking Jimmy if he wanted a beer. The more Jimmy said no, the more Todd pushed.

"Listen," he finally said. "I'll play you a game of eight ball. You win, I stop drinking. I win, you loosen up a little. Okay?"

Jimmy could never turn down competition.

Only it wasn't competition. Todd creamed him, which shouldn't have been a surprise. It was his pool table, and I don't think Jimmy had played pool more than two or three times in his life.

When the match was over, Todd popped open a beer and handed it to Jimmy. I got myself one, too.

I figured on drinking one beer and no more. But it didn't work that way. When Jimmy finished his first, Todd challenged him again. Jimmy lost again, and I found myself drinking a second. After that second beer went down, I didn't think twice about taking a third, a fourth, a fifth. And neither did Jimmy.

I could lie and say I had a miserable time, but the truth is I had fun. We all did. We shot pool and talked about baseball and about girls. I'm not going to write down any of the stuff we said because what I remember seems really stupid, though it didn't seem stupid then.

I didn't pay attention to the time. Neither did Jimmy. When I finally looked at my watch, it was after eleven-thirty. The bus stopped running at midnight, so we had to hustle to catch it. Bouncing around in the back, I started to feel a little sick to my stomach. Jimmy probably felt the same way, because he didn't say one word. When he got off, he barely waved. My head was spinning when I opened my front door. Fortunately, my mother was asleep. I slipped silently down the hall and dropped onto my bed.

I lay there trying to get hold of myself when that first taste of barf worked its way up my throat and into my mouth. I choked it down, but then I belched and it came back stronger. I barely made it to the toilet before I puked my guts out.

I took a shower, then threw my clothes in the wash. When I hit the sack again, it was after one. I dropped right to sleep.

In the morning my head ached, my mouth burned, my stomach churned. And I worried. I was sure my mother had heard me throwing up, or that she'd become suspicious about the load of wash. When that didn't happen, I thought maybe Todd's parents would find the beer bottles and get the names of everyone at the party. The whole morning I lived in dread that everything would blow up in my face.

But it didn't. Nothing happened.

Around noon I headed over to Henry Ford. Jimmy was

102

already there. He gave me a thin smile. "I don't feel much like playing baseball today."

He didn't get any argument from me.

17✦

In June Jimmy took me and Todd Franks to Tom Wells Sports on El Camino. Somehow — probably through his father — Jimmy knew the owner, a nice, older guy with thinning hair and a fat stomach. Anyway, around back was an old pitching machine the San Jose Bees had used. The owner said we could hit for as long as we wanted. "Just don't set the speed above seventy miles an hour," he said before he went back inside. "I don't trust that machine, and I don't want anybody getting hurt."

For Jimmy and Todd it was competition from day one. They'd take turns drilling line drives into the netting. When one of them caught the ball solid, he'd look at the other guy as if to say, "I bet you can't match that." The other guy would step in, and after he'd nailed one, he'd look over with an expression that said, "That was for you."

I wanted to be in on the competition. Maybe I didn't hit the ball as often as they did, but I swung so viciously that when I did hit it, I hit it almost as hard. The crack of my bat driving through the ball was sweet.

In the beginning of the summer Jimmy and Todd kept the machine at seventy just like the owner had said. But in July they started cranking up the speed.

I stayed with them through seventy-five miles an hour,

but around eighty they lost me. When it was my turn, I moved the machine back to seventy-five, and all three of us pretended it didn't matter. But it mattered. It mattered a lot.

So every once in a while I'd hack at pitches coming at eighty. Talk about frustrating. I'd see the ball perfectly; I'd be right on it. Only it would be past me. I'd end up swinging at the breeze.

"Drop the speed," Jimmy would say, and I'd do it, but I felt like a tagalong little brother. By the end of the summer I was so frustrated I was actually glad to be getting back to school and away from that machine.

18♦

On the first day back at Woodside came good news: Sharront was the new head coach of varsity baseball. "He's going to look to the future," Jimmy said. "He'll stack the team with sophomores."

I wanted to believe Jimmy, but I wasn't so sure. "He'll still give the juniors and seniors first shot at everything."

Jimmy brushed that off. "Why should he? Those guys went four and eighteen last year. He doesn't know them. But he knows us. I'm telling you, it's there for the taking."

I wanted to take it. So did Jimmy and Todd. What really ate at us was waiting — the first half of that school year dragged.

School was school. It wasn't like being a freshman, when the honors program was new and scary, and time raced by. As a sophomore I sat in class, did worksheets, studied at home. Then the next day I'd do the same thing. And the next day I'd do the same thing. Sometimes I wondered if baseball season would ever come.

My social life was pretty routine, too. Every week or two Todd would get his hands on some beer and invite Jimmy and me over. We'd shoot pool, talk about girls and baseball, and drink. We didn't get caught, not once in all that time — though we did have a couple of close calls.

The first came the day after Thanksgiving. The buses were running on holiday schedule. Jimmy and I didn't know it, so we ended up stuck on the Alameda at midnight. I had to call my mother to pick us up. The whole ride home she kept asking me if I was sick. "You don't look right," she said.

"I'm just tired," I told her.

She frowned when she looked over her shoulder and saw Jimmy slumped down in the backseat, but she didn't push it.

The second close call came over Christmas break. We were in Todd's room one Tuesday afternoon when his father, who'd come home early from work, knocked on the door. It was bad enough madly trying to hide the beer bottles under chairs and behind the stereo. But the worst part was trying to act calm with his father in the room. Mr. Franks shot pool with us for half an hour or so. He was laughing and joking, and we tried to laugh and joke with him. But Jimmy and I were sweating bullets, and Todd was ten times worse.

If anybody had asked us then if we were big drinkers,

we would have said no. We were baseball players; we were athletes. Drinking didn't fit — we knew it. But Todd got beer whenever he could. And whenever he got it, we drank it.

19♦

I figured that Jimmy's father must have moved away, because all through fall I never saw him. Redwood City isn't that big. If he were around, I'd have run into him at Woodside Plaza or down on the Boardwalk. I suppose I could have asked Jimmy about him, but I figured if Jimmy had anything to say, he'd say it.

That's why what happened that Saturday in January was such a shock. Jimmy and I were hitting grounders to each other at Henry Ford when a bright red Chevy Camaro pulled up. The horn sounded. We looked at each other. "Who's that?" I asked.

"Beats me," Jimmy replied.

A second later Mr. Winter popped out of the car. "I was hoping to find you boys here. You don't mind if an old guy joins in, do you?"

You'd have thought he hadn't been gone a day.

It's hard to say how I felt that afternoon. Mr. Winter was trying to be a good guy, but he overdid it. When Jimmy made a fairly good catch or throw, Mr. Winter acted like he was a Golden Glover. "Put that one on the highlight reel!" . . . "Super slick!" . . . "Awesome!" . . . Corny stuff, like that, over and over — and the opposite of the way he'd always been.

106

Jimmy was dying inside. He was stone-faced the whole two hours his father was there.

That put the pressure on me. I had to be doubly cheerful to make up. Mr. Winter and I grinned away at each other while Jimmy glowered at both of us. The whole thing was weird.

Finally Jimmy couldn't take any more. "I've got some stuff to do," he said. "I'm going home."

His father held up his hands like a traffic cop. "Wait a second. You're not in such a hurry you don't have time for a soft drink." It was kind of sad — he was treating us as if we were still little kids who'd go crazy for a soda.

When Mr. Winter opened his cooler, I expected to see some beer, but there was nothing but Coke. I saw Jimmy stare long and hard at the cooler, too.

Early the next morning Jimmy phoned. "I don't know if you want to meet at Henry Ford today or not. My father might show again. I can't do anything about it. He's always had visiting rights. Now he's in some alcohol treatment program, and he says he wants to get to know me again." Jimmy's voice was filled with anger I didn't understand.

"What's wrong with that?" I asked.

"He won't follow through, Seth. He never does."

A part of me wanted out of the whole thing, but Jimmy was my friend. "I don't care if your father shows. I don't have anything against him."

His father did show. Every Saturday and Sunday for the next month, Mr. Winter smiled his way through a couple hours of baseball, and then pulled out his cooler filled with Cokes. I kept thinking that something had to give, that Jimmy would have to break down and start being nicer, or that Mr. Winter would explode. But nothing changed.

As the weeks rolled by, I found myself more and more on Mr. Winter's side. The way I saw it, Mr. Winter was trying, but Jimmy wouldn't give him a break. I kept thinking there was something I should do. Finally my mother noticed.

"What's wrong, Seth? You seem a million miles away."

I didn't plan on telling her much, but once I started I told her everything, including the fact that I was fed up with Jimmy.

"Seth, you don't know all that's gone on in that house."

That made me angry. "I know Mr. Winter used to drink. But he's stopped. What more does Jimmy want?"

My mother pursed her lips. "I bet Jimmy has seen his father stop drinking a dozen times — minimum. And every time, he's watched his father start again. Once alcohol gets a grip on a person, it's tough to shake free. Ever." She paused. "You remember that for yourself, too."

Instantly my heart raced. "That's not fair," I said. "I'm not into drinking or drugs or anything. Why are you giving me a lecture?"

My mother was startled. "Pretty touchy, aren't you? That was hardly a lecture."

"I'm not touchy," I snapped. "I'm just saying you shouldn't act like . . . like . . . ."

"Like what, Seth?"

"Oh, I don't know." I stood, trying to think of something to say. "Look, I've got homework," I finally managed before retreating to my room.

That Saturday night Jimmy and I were supposed to go to Todd's. At school on Friday I pulled him aside. "We shouldn't be doing this," I said. "It's stupid. If we get caught, Sharront will never let us play varsity."

Jimmy looked puzzled. "We won't get caught."

I sucked up my courage. "Look, isn't it crazy to be down on your father for drinking, and then go out and drink yourself?"

Jimmy's eyes turned mean. "It's not the same at all, Seth. My father drank every single day. I saw him; I lived with him. You didn't. What we're doing isn't anything like what he did."

I started to say something else, but he interrupted. "Don't come if you don't want to." Then he stalked off.

All that day I told myself I wouldn't go. But Saturday afternoon, after Jimmy and I had played a little ball, things looked different.

"The regular time tonight?" I asked.

Jimmy nodded. "The regular time."

20♦

When varsity tryouts finally came, I ached inside. I wanted to make the team, to turn double plays, to score runs, to have a varsity letter on my school jacket. I wanted it just like Jimmy and Todd did. I didn't want to be the one stuck on the junior varsity, the one left out.

I wasn't worried about my fielding. Hitting is what worried me. I was certain I'd do or die at the plate.

Dan Duncan, a junior and my main competition at second, was strictly a banjo hitter. He put the ball in play, moved runners up, bunted pretty well. But he had zero pop in his bat.

During batting practice I muscled up on the pitches I saw. I'm not saying I drove the ball like Jimmy or Todd. Those guys really put on a show. But for a second baseman, I hit a few shots. I whiffed a few, too, but that happens if you swing hard.

Sharront stood behind the cage watching. After I'd really smacked one, I'd peek back. I couldn't read his face. Sometimes it would seem like I'd pound the ball hard, and he'd scowl.

Four days into tryouts, Jimmy pulled me aside. "You're a second baseman," he told me, "you don't have to murder the ball. Just make contact. And you can't let your defense slide."

That got me mad. "I'm not going to make the team hitting ground balls, Jimmy. I've got to make an impression. Besides, I don't see you cutting down on your swing any."

"It's different for me."

That really frosted me. "Why? Why is it different for you? Maybe I'm a better hitter than you think."

He shrugged. "Do what you want, Seth."

That's what I did. I made sure I didn't get cheated when I stepped up to the plate. While Dan Duncan was

110

hitting ground ball after ground ball back up the middle, I was cracking a few off the fences.

Before practice the second Monday, Sharront called out a bunch of names. Mine was one of them. We followed him into the gym conference room.

He put his hands up to quiet us. Then he started pacing around. "Believe me, I know what it feels like to hear this kind of news, so I'm going to spit it out fast. I'm assigning all of you to the junior varsity. Report to Mr. Blackman on field three."

There was a general groan. Sharront clapped his hands. "Hey, listen. I know you boys are disappointed. But don't quit. If you play well, and some varsity player dogs it, I'll move you up and send him down. That's a promise."

Jimmy was waiting outside. "Was that what I think it was?"

I nodded.

Jimmy looked down. "Sorry, Seth," he mumbled. Then he hustled off to field one while I walked over to field three.

Jayvee practice ended half an hour before varsity practice. I'd always hated Sharront's two-mile run, but as I watched the varsity players chug around the track, I would have given anything to have been with them.

I hung around to walk home with Jimmy. I wanted to complain about getting cut; I wanted Jimmy to tell me I'd gotten a raw deal. But before I could say anything, he started telling me about his father.

"He's moving to San Francisco," Jimmy said, "to live with this new woman. He might even marry her

111

someday. It's for sure I won't see much of him anymore.''

"I thought you didn't want to see him anyway," I
said, and I knew I was being mean. "So why do you
care?''

"I don't care," Jimmy said defiantly. "I don't.''

After that we walked silently up the Alameda for a
couple of blocks. I was licking my wounds about being
cut, and I figured Jimmy was thinking about his father.
But he wasn't. It was his mother he was thinking about.
He told me that she'd given up on his father, too.

"That's what you've always wanted, isn't it?" I
asked, still being mean.

"Yeah, I suppose so. Only . . ." He paused. "Seth,
do you think your mother will ever remarry?''

An electric shock jolted my body.

"No.''

"Why not?''

"I don't know," I said, floundering. "I'm just sure
she won't.''

Jimmy looked puzzled. "She's probably lonely, don't
you think? I mean, it makes sense to me she'd want to
get married again. I figure my mother will.''

"Well, my mother isn't going to," I said. "Let's drop
it, okay?''

For the rest of the day, I did everything I could to
keep from thinking about Jimmy's question, but it was
the only thing I could think about.

He was right. It would be natural for my mother to remarry. I don't know why I'd never thought of it before.
Jimmy sure saw it with his mother right away. Maybe

112

I'd blinded myself because I didn't want to face the truth. My mother was smart and she was pretty. She'd have no trouble meeting some man who'd want to marry her. It would be the best thing for her — I knew it.

But that didn't mean I wanted it. I couldn't imagine having some strange man living in our house, giving me orders. Would he expect me to call him "Dad"? Just the thought of it made my head pound.

Part Three

1♦

I hated being on the junior varsity. For one thing, I barely talked to Jimmy. We didn't even eat lunch together. He sat with Todd and other guys on the varsity. I didn't fit there, and I didn't want to eat with the junior-varsity guys, so I ate by myself. And after a couple of days I stopped hanging around waiting for Jimmy's practice to end. It was too humiliating. Jimmy and I couldn't meet at Henry Ford on weekends either. My games were on Saturday afternoon; his were on Sunday. It wasn't his fault; it wasn't my fault. It was just the way it was.

The junior varsity practiced on the field right across from the varsity. Every once in a while I'd hear the crack of a bat meeting the ball absolutely perfectly, and with power, on the varsity diamond. I'd turn and look, and sure enough it would be Jimmy or Todd in the batting cage.

When either one caught the ball on the screws like that, it would roll all the way onto our field, sometimes right to me at second base. Coach Blackman would call

114

time, and I'd have to pick the ball up and toss it to a varsity outfielder. I felt like I was a servant then, and they were my masters. Practicing near them was like picking at a scab — the wound won't heal.

Once the season started, I grew more miserable — if that's possible. Jimmy and Todd both got off to hot starts. It seemed like every game they were banging out extra-base hits, driving in runs, and making sensational plays in the field.

Then something happened that made me feel totally left out. One Monday afternoon I was by my locker dressing. Jimmy and Todd were maybe twenty feet away, talking real loud and laughing. I couldn't help overhearing. It turned out they'd had a big party, a kegger up at Huddart Park.

I'd been wanting to quit drinking, so I shouldn't have cared about not having been invited. But I did care. I felt completely abandoned. Being stuck on the junior varsity was like not existing. I had to get myself moved up to the varsity. I had to.

If there was an opening, I figured Sharront would call up the jayvee player with the best batting average. So I focused on my swing. I'm not saying I didn't play any defense at all. I fielded okay. Maybe I didn't dive for grounders up the middle, and maybe I didn't back up every throw. But it's hard to do that stuff on the jayvees.

I can't remember much about any of the games during the first half of that season. I think our record was 3-5, or maybe even 2-6. The truth is I didn't care. All I cared about was my batting average.

People talk about how baseball is a team sport, but

115

that's exaggerated. You can go whole games, sometimes two or three in a row, when all you have to do is look out for yourself. You get a base hit, you're helping your batting average and you're helping your team. But every once in a while baseball is a team game. And when those times roll around, not being a team player hurts.

Our ninth game that year was against Sequoia. With the scored tied 1–1 in the bottom of the sixth, I came up with a runner on second and nobody out. In that situation, the batter's job is to move the runner to third.

The best way to advance a runner is to hit a ground ball to the right side of the infield. If it goes through for a hit, great. But if it doesn't, the first baseman or the second baseman is going to field it. They'd have to throw all the way across the diamond to cut down the base runner going from second to third. That's a long throw and a bad bet, so ninety-nine times out of a hundred they go to first with the ball and make the sure out. The base runner takes third, and from third he can often score on an out.

But if you give yourself up, you get zip in the scorecard. You don't get a hit, you don't even get credit for a sacrifice. You set it up for someone else, and only your teammates appreciate what you've done.

The first pitch was a curveball on the outside part of the plate, a perfect pitch to pound into the ground over toward first. I could have done it, or at least taken a shot at doing it, but I let that pitch go by. I wasn't looking to set things up for somebody else. I was looking for a game-winning RBI, something that Sharront would hear about. I was looking to set things up for me.

I worked the count to 3-2 before I got what I was waiting for — a fastball down the pike. I turned on it, and I hit a screaming line drive, but right at the third baseman. He gloved it without moving a step. The ball was hit so hard they doubled up the runner easily. Instead of one out with a man on third, we had two out and nobody on. Our next hitter smacked a high fly to deep center. If we'd had a runner on third, he would have scored easily.

We lost the game in extra innings. Coach Blackman didn't say anything to me, and neither did any of the other guys. But I could read the looks on their faces, and I felt like an insect.

As soon as I dragged myself in the door that night, my mother told me Jimmy had called. That perked me up a little. I phoned him right back.

"Hey, Seth," he said, sounding real excited. "Did you see the *Tribune* tonight?"

I hadn't.

"Well look at it, old buddy. Page C-4."

I put the telephone down and picked up the newspaper from the kitchen table. I flipped to C-4. I didn't know what I was looking for, so it took a second to find it. But once I saw it, my heart raced. There was a photo of Jimmy and Todd, bats crossed. The headline above it said "Woodside's Bruise Brothers."

I picked up the phone. "That's great, Jimmy," I said, trying hard to be happy for him.

His voice was full of joy. "You've got to read it, too.

A Baltimore scout says I remind him of Cal Ripken. Didn't I tell you I'd be a major leaguer someday? Didn't I?"

"Yeah, you sure did."

Jimmy didn't stop, but I can't tell you what more he said. I just stared at his picture in the paper and said "Yeah" every once in a while. I was jealous — there's no other word for it. But before he hung up he said something I did hear loud and clear.

"By the way, it looks like Randy Driscoll's going to need shoulder surgery. So play hard, Seth. Sharront will be bringing somebody up."

I got it in my head that how I did against Saratoga on Saturday would decide everything. That made me tight, and when you're tight, you're lousy. My first at bat I swung at a pitch a foot over my head, and then was caught looking at a fastball right down the heart of the plate. The next two times up I went fishing for low, outside curveballs and grounded out.

In the field I was terrible, too, mainly because I kept thinking about my pathetic at bats, and how a hitless day would ruin my chances of being moved to the varsity. I butchered a grounder in the third inning, and the guy eventually scored. And in the fifth I just plain didn't get over to cover second on a steal. The catcher's throw sailed into center, and the runner ended up at third. He scored, too, on a squeeze bunt.

We were down three runs when we came up in the seventh for our last at bat. I led off. The pitcher was losing it. His first pitch was way outside, and he grunted like a tennis player as he released the ball. His second pitch was in the dirt. The third pitch was closer, but it was still outside by a good six inches.

I stepped out of the box, tugged on my batting gloves.

Most 3-0 pitches are easy to hit, fastballs down the pike with not much on them. But when your team is down three runs with nobody on base, you don't swing, ever. One run doesn't win the game, and no matter how hard you hit a ball, there's always the chance somebody will catch it.

I knew if I looked down toward third base, Blackman would flash me the take sign. It was automatic.

So I didn't look.

I stepped back in. The pitcher delivered a nothing pitch, a batting-practice special. I swung from the heels and caught the ball sweet. It was gone the second I hit it, a towering fly ball way over the left-field fence.

Saratoga's coach brought in a reliever, and he shut us down; 3–1 was the final score.

After the game Blackman came over. "You really pounded that one, Barham."

"It was nice to spoil the shutout," I said.

His eyes went steely. "The thing is, I had the take sign on."

I flushed. "I'm sorry, Coach. I forgot to look."

"A smart kid like you. Honors program. And you forgot?"

I bluffed it out. "I forgot. Honest."

He looked me in the eye until I had to look away.

*   *   *

Monday Jimmy spotted me in the hall before school. "Driscoll goes in for surgery today," he said, as he hustled off to his class. Then he turned back. "I heard about your home run. See you on field one today!"

The instant I opened the door to the locker room, Sharront called me to his office. The adrenaline surged — I felt like I was up with the bases loaded. But when I stepped into his office, Sharront didn't seem happy. "Sit down, Barham," he muttered.

He fumbled with some papers, tugged at his beard. "So tell me, Barham, why are you suddenly acting like a kid with a bad attitude?"

I was stunned. "What do you mean?"

He leaned back in his chair, raised his hands above his head. "What do I mean? I saw it in tryouts. Swinging for the fences; dogging it in the field. You weren't the same kid who played freshman ball. That's why I cut you. I was hoping it would wake you up."

He pulled on his beard again. "But Coach Blackman says you don't back up bases; you don't give yourself up to advance runners. Saturday you hit away on a three-oh pitch with your team down three runs. What's going through your head?"

"Nothing's going through my head," I stammered.

He laughed mockingly. "I'd say that's true."

I wanted to sink under the table.

Sharront sighed. "Listen, Barham. Last year you impressed me with your hustle and your baseball smarts. I figured you for my starting second baseman by the time you were a senior. But you don't hustle, you don't play smart, and you won't make varsity. Not this year, not next year, not any year." He stopped. "Is my message coming through?"

I managed to nod.

"Good. Now here is what's going to happen. Coach Blackman is going to sit you on the bench for a couple of games. You use that time as a gut check. Think about whether you want to be a ballplayer or not. And if you don't want to be, then quit."

He put his head down and started writing something. I waited a minute or so.

"Can I go now?" I finally asked.

He didn't even look up. "Yeah, go."

I saw Jimmy across the locker room before practice. He opened his hands as if to say, "So what happened?" I shook my head. "Sorry," he mouthed.

I stayed up late that night doing homework, trying to work myself into exhaustion so I'd be able to sleep. But it didn't work. I tossed and turned. At two o'clock I turned the lamp back on, grabbed my glove, and started pounding a baseball into the pocket.

My mind raced. Who was Sharront trying to kid? When he was in the minors, was he Mr. Team Player? Or did he swing away every once in a while hoping to catch the eye of the major-league teams? That's all I was trying to do — catch his eye. And since when was hitting a home run such a bad thing?

I kept pounding the ball into my glove, feeling more and more sorry for myself. But way in the back of my brain another thought was buzzing around. No matter how many times I pounded that ball into my glove, the thought wouldn't go away.

Sharront was right. Blackman was right. I'd been playing stupid. Selfish and stupid.

I took a deep breath, exhaled. Then I flicked off the light, rolled over, and fell asleep. Finally.

2♦

But bad habits are hard to shake. I vowed that for the rest of the season I was going to dive for balls, back up throws, take extra bases — do everything the way I used to.

And I tried. I'd be completely into the game for two, three innings. Then I'd space out a little, get a bad jump on a pop to short right or not anticipate a drag bunt.

When I'd get caught napping, I'd feel like an A-1 idiot. Coach Blackman didn't ride me, though. "The effort is there, Seth," he said after I'd screwed up a rundown. "That's the important thing."

I'd also forgotten how hard hustling is on the body. As the season wore on, I had more and more bruises. Sometimes I'd be so sore it would hurt to take a practice swing.

Playing for the junior varsity is hard on the mind, too. Nobody came to our games. Sometimes I'd spot the umpires peeking at their watches. It was like playing in a black hole.

Still, we won our last four games to end up with a 9-9 record. I'd like to think that my play had something to do with that. After the last game Coach Blackman told us to be proud of the way we'd fought back, and it seemed like he was looking right at me when he said it. All that time I'd kept totally focused on my jayvee games. But once our season was over, I let myself pay attention to the varsity. If they could beat St. Francis, they would finish first and take a spot in the state tournament.

The deciding game was Sunday. Banners were pinned up in the hallways around the school. Kids cleared a path for Jimmy and Todd whenever either walked down the hall. The "Bruise Brothers" thing had really caught on, mainly because the two of them kept pounding the ball. Jimmy was number one in batting average at .448, and Todd led in home runs and runs batted in. At school Friday there was a big pep rally. You could feel the excitement roll down off the bleachers.

Sunday morning I headed up to Woodside an hour before the game. I wanted to get a seat behind home plate, and I wanted to say something to Jimmy. I don't know what, but something.

When I reached the field, the St. Francis guys were playing pepper, catching fungoes, stretching. Our varsity was nowhere to be seen. I figured Sharront was giving the guys a last-minute pep talk, so I settled into a seat in the bleachers and waited.

As the minutes ticked away, I had a strong feeling something was wrong. Cory Russell, our starting pitcher, should have been in the bullpen throwing. Sharront wouldn't cut so deep into warm-ups for a pep talk.

Fifteen minutes before game time, the locker-room
123

doors opened and the team finally took the field. But nothing seemed right. The players were walking, for one thing, and their heads were hanging. I couldn't see either Jimmy or Todd.

A guy in my French class tapped me on the shoulder. "Barham, you know Winter, don't you? Did something happen to him?"

I shook my head. "Not that I know of."

But I suspected. Right away I suspected.

3♦

For the first two innings of that game, the talk in the stands was about Jimmy and Todd. All kinds of theories were tossed around.

In the top of the third the answer came, and it was what I'd been afraid of. I don't know who found out, or how, but the news raced through the bleachers. Jimmy and Todd had gotten drunk the night before. Sharront had found out, and he'd suspended them.

Immediately arguments broke out.

"What clowns!" one girl said. "Screwing up everything for everybody."

"Sharront's the clown," a guy answered her. "So they had some beer. Big deal. Like they're the only ones who ever drink. Sharront could have had them run some extra laps or something. He didn't have to suspend them."

"Extra laps," the girl scoffed. "As if that's anything."

So it went, back and forth, all around me. I tried to

124

tune out the arguments, but it was impossible. So I climbed from the bleachers and found a spot down the right-field line where I could stand by myself.

I barely watched the game. I kept thinking about Jimmy and Todd, about how they'd blown it for the whole team, how they'd blown it for themselves. I wondered what they were doing. I almost went to the locker room to look for them, but I figured that even if they were there, they wouldn't want to see anyone.

When I looked up at the scoreboard, the game was in the top of the seventh and was still scoreless. St. Francis's second baseman led off. He was a little guy — no power at all. Sharront had the outfield playing shallow and pulled around to the right.

Maybe Russell was tired. Or maybe he figured the guy couldn't hit. Whatever the reason, his first pitch was a curveball out over the middle of the plate. The St. Francis hitter ripped the ball down the first-base line. It kicked around in the corner, and the batter made third base with a headfirst slide.

Sharront had no choice. He motioned for the infield to come in tight. On a 2-2 pitch, Russell jammed the St. Francis hitter. The batter got a little wood on the ball, and flared a pop to short right. Had Duncan been at normal depth, he would have caught it. But playing in, he had no chance. The ball landed in shallow right field, the saddest excuse for an RBI single I've ever seen. That one run was all they got, but it was one more run than we had.

Devon Maxwell led off the bottom of the seventh for us. He crowded the plate, exaggerating his crouch in order to shrink the strike zone. He worked the count to 3-2, then fouled one off. Will Whitmore, St. Francis's hurler, stepped up to the rubber, delivered. It was a fastball on the inside part of the plate. I could see the ump start to raise his right hand, then pull it down. Ball four. We had the leadoff batter on.

Sharront put the bunt on, and Duncan got it down perfectly, putting Maxwell at second with one out. The three and four spots in the lineup were up. A single from either player would tie the game.

The St. Francis manager took the slow walk to the mound. He talked to Whitmore a little, then motioned to the bullpen. I knew who was coming in. Everybody knew who was coming in. Steve Cannon.

It should have been great. No matter how it played out, it should have been something to see. Our best against their best. Jimmy Winter vs. Steve Cannon . . . Todd Franks vs. Steve Cannon. Fastball hitters against a fastball pitcher, with the title on the line. But it had been ruined. Instead of Jimmy and Todd we had Vaughn and Pacheco.

Way out where I was I could hear Cannon's first pitch smack into the catcher's glove. "Strike one!" the umpire yelled. I could have left right then, but I stayed and watched it all. Six pitches, six strikes. Cannon blew both Vaughn and Pacheco away.

4♦

"That's too bad," my mother said when I told her the final score. "How did Jimmy do?"

"He didn't play. He must have missed practice or something. Sharront suspended him."

She looked puzzled. "He missed practice before a championship game?"

I scrambled for an answer. "I'm not exactly sure what he did. Maybe he cut class or something. Sharront's real strict."

That seemed to satisfy her. At least she didn't ask any more questions.

About eight-thirty that night the doorbell rang. I flicked on the light and saw Jimmy standing on the front porch. "You feel like going for a walk?" he asked.

We headed to Stulsaft Park. For the first block or so he didn't say anything. "Did you hear what happened?" he finally asked.

"Sort of," I replied. "The word was you and Todd got caught drinking."

He didn't answer.

"Is that right?" I asked. "Is that what happened?"

"Yeah, that's what happened."

When we reached Stulsaft, we sat under a gnarled oak tree. Jimmy pulled a blade of grass out of the ground and chewed on the sweet white part. I did the same. The sun was down, but the night was warm.

"It was a good game," I said.

"That's what I hear." He paused. "You didn't happen to see any major-league scouts there, did you?"

I shrugged. "I don't know. I don't know what scouts look like."

"They look like anybody, only they have notebooks and write stuff down all the time."

127

"I didn't see anybody writing anything down."

He grimaced. "They were there. I'm sure of it. And there's the All-League team — I might not make that now." He slumped forward. "I can't believe this."

"What happened?" I asked.

He sighed. "I can hardly tell you, I feel so stupid. We were going to shoot pool and drink a few beers, but then I thought, why not the bleachers?"

"At Woodside? You were drinking right at school?"

"I felt like being at the park. I don't know why. I just did."

"So who caught you? Is there a night watchman or something?"

Jimmy managed a weak laugh. "Sharront caught us. God knows what he was doing there or how he heard us. We weren't making any noise. But he was on us before we knew it. Flashlight in the face, phone call to the parents, the police, the vice principal. The joke is I don't think either of us had more than two swigs of beer."

"What were you thinking, Jimmy? It's crazy to be drinking the night before a big game."

He gave me a look of pure disgust. "Come on, Seth, don't you start, too. Todd got some beer so we were going to drink it. Okay? If I'd asked you, you would have come with us in a minute."

"That's not true," I said.

His eyes flashed. "Seth, name one time, just one time, when you turned down a beer."

I didn't answer. I couldn't.

5♦

The last week in May Jimmy and Todd were both named to the All-League team. I grabbed Jimmy in the hall and congratulated him. "I was afraid Sharront would keep us off somehow," he said, smiling. "I'm sure glad he didn't. I'll be playing tournaments all summer. Scouts will be crawling all over the place."

Three weeks later final grades came out. I made high honors. My mother was ecstatic. "I'm so proud of you. High honors is quite an accomplishment."

For a treat, she took me to Harry's Hofbrau. I got a barbecued steak and jumbo fries, stuff we never had at home. "You don't seem happy," she said. "Is something wrong?"

I was proud of what I'd done. But it wasn't like making All-League. Not by a long shot. I couldn't tell her that, though. She would have said that good grades were more important, and she would have kept after me until she forced me to agree.

That summer I wangled a job caddying at Menlo Country Club. I also signed up for driver's ed, and a keyboarding class. "You're not going to have any spare time," my mother warned me. "When are you going to see your friends?"

I shrugged her off. I really didn't expect to see Jimmy that summer. He'd be playing in tournaments all over the state. And when he was in town, I figured, he'd probably hang out with Todd and other guys from the varsity.

Jimmy surprised me, though. Whenever he was around for a few days, he'd drop by the house. I'd ask him how his games were going, and we'd talk a little baseball.

He didn't brag. Jimmy wasn't that way. Still, it was clear that he was making the plays in the field and getting his hits.

When he was with me, I was excited for him. But after he left, I'd sometimes get real down. It seemed like he was having the most exciting summer of his life, while I was having the most boring one of mine.

I didn't pick up a ball or a glove or a bat all through June or the early part of July. Talking to Jimmy once in a while wasn't enough. I missed the game. It was almost like being sick or something. So in mid-July I started taking the bus to Tom Wells once I'd finished caddying. The first time, I felt strange going in there alone, like I was a loser because I was by myself. I was also afraid the owner wouldn't remember me. But his face lit up the second he saw me.

"It's been a mite too quiet around here," he said. "There's no prettier sound in the world than a bat hitting a ball." I tried to give him money, but he wouldn't take it.

I started with the machine set at seventy miles an hour. I figured if I just tried to meet the ball, I'd get around better on fastballs. My plan was to crank the machine up one mph every week. That would put me around eighty miles an hour by the end of the summer. If I could keep moving it up little by little, I'd be able to handle all but the fastest pitchers, the Steve Cannons. Deep down I hoped someday I'd be able to handle even them.

For a while I was right on schedule. By August 10, I
130

had the machine up to seventy-nine. I struggled that day, but I didn't worry. People always say you can do whatever you set your mind to do, if you're willing to work at it. I was willing to work.

So I went back the next day, and the day after, and the day after that. Each time I set the machine at seventy-nine, and each time those fastballs ate me up. After a week, I was so depressed I barely touched my dinner.

"I've never known you to leave spaghetti uneaten," my mother said. "What's the problem?"

"Oh, it's just something with my swing. You wouldn't understand."

"Try me."

I figured she'd keep after me until I told her, so I spilled it. "But I'm going to stay with it," I said when I'd finished. "I'm not going to quit."

"I admire the way you stick to things, Seth," she said. "I really do. But have you ever thought that maybe you've reached your limit?"

I felt myself go cold. "Don't say that. You're going to jinx me."

She spoke softly. "It's nothing to be ashamed of. Everybody has a limit."

"I haven't reached my limit," I snapped. "Not by a long shot."

"Okay, okay. Forget I said anything."

But I couldn't. As I stared down the pitching machine the next day, I felt as if she were watching. I was going to show her. I set the machine to seventy-nine. I opened my eyes wide; every nerve in my body was tense, ready.

There it was, a fastball down the heart of the plate. I

131

saw it perfectly; I brought my hands forward, shifted my weight to my front foot as I pushed off the back. I had the knob of the bat right at my belt buckle; my head was down. Everything was right.

But I whiffed it. I was on the ball, but late. Not once, but every single time. Over and over.

6♦

Right before school started, Jimmy stopped by the house. We sat at the kitchen table and ate peanuts.

"That's it," he said. "No more tournaments this summer." He shook his head. "I'm sure going to miss playing. And I'm going to hate being cooped up in some classroom again."

"School's not so bad," I said.

He threw his head back. "For you it isn't. But I can't believe I've still got two more years before I graduate."

After that we talked about nothing for a while. I turned the radio to the Giants game. Jimmy wasn't listening though. I could tell there was something he wanted to say, but couldn't bring out.

Finally he said, "Listen, Seth, my father is getting married Saturday. Up in Portola Valley at some little chapel. He said I could invite one person, and I was wondering . . . you know . . ." His voice trailed off.

"I'm not doing anything, Jimmy," I said. "I'll go."

Saturday at noon Jimmy pulled up in front of my house in his father's red Camaro. My mother panicked. "I
132

didn't know Jimmy was going to drive,'' she said as he was walking to the front door.

I razzed her. "Once they post my grade for driver's ed, I'll be getting my license. We're not little boys."

"I know. But those roads up to Portola Valley are tricky."

"Oh, Mom," I said, "don't worry."

When Jimmy came in, she started with the advice. "Cars on those mountain roads veer out . . ." I didn't think she'd ever stop.

"I'm sorry," I said to Jimmy when we finally made it out of the house.

"Don't sweat it," he said. "My mother is the same way."

On Woodside Road, we got stuck behind some old Plymouth Valiant poking up the hill. Jimmy pulled out, put the pedal to the floor. The Camaro zoomed past.

"What do you think of my car?"

"Your car?" I said, not sure I'd heard him right.

He nodded. "Yeah. My father gave it to me."

"You're kidding."

"No joke. I think he feels guilty about getting married again. He's trying to make up." He popped a cassette into the tape deck. "Check out the sound system."

It took half an hour to get to the chapel, and the wedding lasted all of ten minutes. I'd thought the woman Mr. Winter was marrying would be young and maybe a little sexy, like the women I'd seen him with, but she wasn't. Her name was Elizabeth Strong. She worked in San Francisco as an X-ray technician and she played the violin. She had silver-black hair and a proud face. When

133

she said "I do" her voice was loud and clear.

At the reception she came over to where Jimmy and I were sitting. I stood, shook her hand. "I hear you're quite a student," she said, which threw me off, because I couldn't figure why she'd ever be talking about me. But she had kind eyes, and she didn't treat me like I was ten years old. When she left I told Jimmy I liked her.

"She's okay," he said. "She doesn't try too hard to be big buddies with me. The big mystery is why she's marrying my father."

We milled around, sipping Cokes, eating sandwiches. Finally Jimmy's father and his new wife cut the cake. A little later they drove off, horn honking.

"Let's get out of here," Jimmy said as soon as the car disappeared around the corner.

When we reached the Camaro, he stopped. "I've got an idea. Wait here a second." He ran into the hall. When he came back he had something wrapped up in a towel. "At least the afternoon won't be a total waste," he said, laughing. He pulled the towel back and showed me a couple of bottles of champagne.

I should have said something right then and there. Maybe that would have kept the rest from happening. But I didn't. I didn't even think of saying anything.

Jimmy took a hard right off Mountain Home Road and drove up a fire trail. "This is a good place," he said. "Nobody can see us from the road."

The champagne went down easy. It was great to sit in the cool shade underneath the oak trees and silently sip from that ice-cold bottle. As we passed the champagne back and forth, a pleasant numbness came over me.

134

After he popped the cork on the second bottle, Jimmy leaned his head back, closed his eyes. "You know something, Seth," he said. "This summer, playing those all-star teams, I studied every shortstop. And not one of them was as good as me. Not one. None of them hit as good as me; none of them fielded like I do. I was the best of the best." He opened his eyes, looked at me. "Does that sound like bragging?"

I sipped some champagne, passed the bottle back to him. "It's not bragging to tell the truth."

He took a swig, shook his head. "My father's the reason I'm so good. Without him I'd be nothing."

"I don't know about that," I said. "You'd be good even without him. You're a natural."

He sort of snickered. "Yeah, maybe I'd be good. But not like I am. Not the best." There was a strange smile on his face. "I'm going to be a major leaguer, Seth. And my father, the biggest jerk in the world, is the reason." He paused. "Life sure is crazy, isn't it?"

I thought about my own father, about the influence he would have had on my life. If he'd lived, I'd be a different person. There is no doubt about it. But how? How would I be different? What parts of me would he have brought into the light? And what parts of me would he have darkened? That is the mystery.

"It sure is," I said at last. "It sure is."

I chugged some more champagne, passed the bottle to him. He finished it off.

We sat there for a good ten minutes, listening to the wind in the trees, thinking our own thoughts. Finally Jimmy started the car. When he took off down Mountain

Home Road, he burned rubber for at least a hundred yards.

Somehow Jimmy made it back. I say *somehow*, because I know I couldn't have. I felt seasick. My knees were wobbly; my ears were ringing.

Once I was home, my mother asked the typical questions and I gave her the typical answers. Or I thought I did. But after a few minutes, she stared at me hard. "Seth, you're drunk."

"I am not drunk," I said, fighting to act normal.

"Oh yes you are," she answered coolly.

"I only had one glass of champagne," I insisted.

"Being drunk is bad enough. Don't be a liar too."

"I tell you I'm not drunk. I only had one, or maybe two, glasses of champagne. That's all."

She glared. "Go to your room, young man. I don't even want to look at you."

I was fuming when I slammed my bedroom door shut and hopped onto my bed. I hated being called a liar. I hated being called a drunk. And the fact that I was drunk, and that I was a liar, made me hate it even more.

I tried to read the sports page, but the words kept jumping around on the page. I lay back and closed my eyes.

When I awoke it was two in the morning. My head ached and my throat was incredibly dry. I was hungry, but the thought of eating made me gag. I took a long shower, then crawled back to bed. I didn't think I'd be able to sleep, but I did.

* * *

My mother was waiting for me at the breakfast table.

"Don't tell me. Let me guess. You have the twenty-four-hour flu."

I'd never heard her more sarcastic.

"No," I answered. "I was drunk."

She sipped her coffee. "Well, at least you admit it. That's something. Not a whole lot, but something. I suppose Jimmy got drunk, too."

I nodded.

She took a deep breath. "I've been thinking about this all night, Seth. Here's what's going to happen." She paused, took another sip of coffee. "First, you're clearly not old enough to handle the responsibility of a driver's license. So you will not get your license when your grade is posted."

I swallowed. "When will I get it?" I asked.

"We'll let six months go by, and then we'll talk again."

Six months was bad, but I was afraid she was going to say a year, or even two.

"And there's another thing. For as long as you live in this house, you are not — I repeat — *not* to get in a car if Jimmy Winter is driving."

"Oh, Mother," I said. "It's not like he's drunk all the time."

Her eyes got that fiery look that I've seen only a few times in my life. "Do you think you've got another life in the bank that you can go get if you lose this one? Do you think I've got another son hidden in some closet? You are not to get in a car with that boy again! Understood?"

137

It was pointless to argue. "Okay. I won't go anywhere with Jimmy if he's driving. Does that make you happy?"

"No," she replied. "None of this makes me happy."

That sentence got to me. It wasn't so much the words she said, but the way she said them. She sounded more than hurt; she sounded wounded.

All day I felt miserable. She'd raised me. By herself she'd raised me. She'd taught me right from wrong, and she'd trusted me to do right. And I'd let her down.

It's never going to happen again, I vowed to myself. *It's never going to happen again.*

And then that night at dinner — at the moment in my life when I least wanted to argue with my mother — we argued.

"I've been thinking," she said, "that maybe you need a man's influence in your life. How would you feel if I called Big Brothers and —"

I broke in right there. "No," I said, shaking my head. "No, nothing like that. You can't do that. I absolutely don't want anything like that."

"But couldn't you try just once, Seth?" she pleaded. "How could it hurt? Just once, that's all I'm asking."

I put my hands to my head. "Mother," I said, "I won't do it. It's impossible."

She closed her eyes for a long time. When she opened them, they were filled with tears. "Sometimes I feel as if you want me to do the impossible. I can't be both mother and father to you, Seth."

"I know you can't, Mother," I answered softly. "And I'm not asking you to be. I just want you to be my mother."

138

"And you won't let me call?"

I shook my head.

She took a deep breath. "All right, I won't." She paused. "Let's eat dinner."

I still feel rotten whenever I think about that conversation. Sometimes I think I should have let my mother call Big Brothers, that I should have gone one time like she wanted. But what would have been the point? I would have just had to say no later.

Maybe some guys in my situation would have wanted a man to be a second father to them. But I didn't. My father is dead. I barely remember him. But nobody is ever going to take his place.

7♦

Jimmy and I didn't do much together that year at Woodside High. We were friends. I felt it every time I saw him. But we had different places in school. I was just one of the kids. Jimmy was a big man on campus. Todd too. The freshmen and sophomores looked up to the two of them like they were gods.

And why not? Everyone had seen the Bruise Brothers article in the newspaper; everyone had at least heard about the home runs and the great catches. They were both going to be major-league stars — famous millionaires. Nobody blamed them much for blowing the chance for the playoffs. Drinking was part of the package — like Jose Canseco with his fast cars.

That year Woodside's football and basketball teams

139

were both lousy. But baseball was going to be different. The whole community was revved up. The *Tribune* ran another feature on Todd and Jimmy. "Bound for Glory" was the headline this time. The writer blabbed on and on about how great both of them were. But the last sentences jumped out at me. "Watching Jimmy Winter now must be what it was like to have watched Honus Wagner when he was sixteen. The boy was born to play baseball, and he'll be playing it for a long, long time." Jimmy must have loved reading that.

A couple of weeks before tryouts, I got my license. "You promise me you'll never drink and drive," my mother said the day I took the driving test.

"I promise," I said. "It won't happen."

"You give me your word."

"I give you my word."

All winter I'd been banging the ball off the back of the house whenever I had a chance. But I hadn't swung the bat at all. It took too long to get down to Tom Wells on the bus. But once I could drive, I could get down there for a half-hour right after dinner.

The first couple of times I kept the machine at seventy. I was hitting the ball pretty solid. So I moved it to seventy-five. Still no problem. I start getting excited then, thinking that maybe my bat had gotten quicker. A couple of days before tryouts, I pushed the machine up to eighty. I had to find out.

I had a good cut at the first ball, and I got a piece of it. I took a deep breath, waited for the next pitch. I saw it perfectly, uncoiled . . . and missed. A lump rose in my throat. *No big deal,* I told myself. *That's why you*
140

get three. Then came another swing . . . another miss. Then a foul tick. Then two more swings and two more misses before another tiny tick. I ended up spending an hour to find out all over again that I couldn't hit a fastball in the eighties.

Instead of going right home, I drove to Mountain Home Road and cranked the radio up full blast. The red rays of the setting sun were sneaking through the green leaves of the trees. It was strange and beautiful at the same time.

Right then, flying down that road with the radio blasting, I stopped kidding myself. All that stuff you hear about being able to do whatever you want to do if you're willing to work at it — it's garbage. I knew it in my bones.

I thought about the great players — Mays, Mantle, Ruth, Koufax, Ryan. They didn't earn their talent. You can't earn talent. It was given to them. Just like it was given to Todd and Jimmy. But it wasn't given to me. Not enough of it, anyway.

I was depressed, but then my depression gave way to. a strange exhilaration. I thought about how my father had described himself. *The best lousy golfer in the world.* Suddenly I knew what he'd meant. Compared to Jimmy and Todd I was lousy. I'd always be lousy. High-school baseball was as far as I was ever going to go. But I was determined to be the best lousy baseball player I could possibly be.

8♦

That spring during tryouts I laid my body on the line to keep every ground ball I could in the infield. I backed up every throw, gave it my all on every foul ball down the line, every bloop into shallow right or center. At the plate, I kept my swing short and sweet. Ground balls and line drives — just like Mr. Winter had told me way back in sixth grade.

The second Monday Sharront called us all together. "If you hear your name, follow me to the conference room of the gym."

I went a little light-headed as he rattled off names. It seemed like the list went on forever. Finally Sharront marched off, the guys whose names he'd called trudging behind.

I looked around. Jimmy was there, so were Todd and Cory Russell and Fred Pacheco and Dan Duncan. And I was there, too. Jimmy put his arm around my shoulder. "Hey, teammate."

I don't remember practice, the two-mile run, walking home. All I remember is an incredible floating feeling, and a sense that somehow my body wasn't big enough to hold the joy surging inside me. I had made the varsity.

Part Four

1♦

Before our opening game, Sharront called me to his office. "Barham, I had you pegged as my utility guy this year. But the plain fact is you've outhit, outfielded, and outhustled Duncan. Which is another way of saying that second base is yours." He stood, shook my hand. "You've come a long way from last year, Seth. A long way."

I was sky-high, but I knew Duncan wouldn't take being benched lightly. He'd push himself harder. And Sharront wouldn't wait on me. A slump, a few errors, and I'd be riding the pines.

That night the *Tribune* predicted we'd take first in our league. The writer said Jimmy and Todd might carry us to the state title.

I bet every guy on the team cringed when he read that. I know I did. Nobody wants to be picked for first. You win and all you've done is what you're supposed to do. Finish second and you've had a lousy year.

We opened on Sunday afternoon with a road game against Carlmont. Warming up, I was so nervous I

143

thought I'd never be able to play. I was trying to wrap my mind around everything that was coming — twenty-two games of batting, fielding, running. Little black spots danced before my eyes, and my ears started ringing.

Jimmy sensed what was happening, and he pulled me through. He asked me questions, forcing me to think about one thing at a time. Was the infield soft or hard? What direction was the wind blowing? How much foul ground behind first base?

Those questions killed the time before the game. Suddenly the umpire yelled, "Play ball!"; Devon Maxwell stood in to lead off; I took my place in the on-deck circle. The waiting was over.

Maxwell took a strike, then a ball, then hit a loud foul to left. On the 1-2 pitch, he popped to second.

"Go get him," Jimmy said to me.

It hurt to swallow — that's how dry my throat was.

Carlmont's pitcher started me with a slow curve outside, then came back with a fastball strike. I fouled off the next fastball, then watched another curve dive into the dirt. The 2-2 pitch was a change-up that froze me. If it had been a strike, I'd have been caught looking, but it was high. I fouled a fastball into the screen, then drew a base on balls on a curve a foot outside. "Way to go, Seth," Sharront hollered from the third-base coach's box. He made me feel like I'd hit a home run.

Jimmy worked the count to 2-1. I looked toward third; Sharront flashed the hit-and-run sign. As I raced toward second I peeked over to make sure Jimmy hadn't popped up. The pitch was two feet outside. There was nothing

144

Jimmy could do for me; I was on my own.

A good peg would have nailed me, but the catcher's throw short-hopped the second baseman and the ball skipped into center field. I scrambled to my feet and took third without a throw. I was ninety feet from scoring my first run. And our big sticks — Jimmy and Todd — were both going to have a shot at knocking me in.

The infield stayed back, willing to give up the run for an out. Jimmy blistered a drive down the third-base line that landed just foul. He returned to the batter's box, but he'd used up his best swing. He struck out on a curveball in the dirt.

We needed a clutch hit from Todd. But he got under a fastball and lifted a routine fly that Carlmont's left fielder hauled in. Sharront clapped his hands. "All right, time to play some 'D.' "

It's hard to describe how incredible it felt to take the field with Jimmy in a varsity game. All those hours of talk — and it had come true. Our first baseman, Bob DeRego, threw us grounders while Cory Russell took his warm-up tosses. When Russell finished, Lance Johnson, our catcher, fired a bullet down to me at second. The ball went around the infield, and then back to Russell. Before the first batter stepped in, Jimmy tossed a little dirt in the air. "Wind's shifting," he called. I nodded. Jimmy nodded back. Then we both smiled.

Carlmont's leadoff hitter laid down a bunt on a 2-1 pitch and caught Dan Hill, our third baseman, flat-footed. The Carlmont guy beat it out without a throw. It didn't faze Russell. He struck out the two hitter and popped up the number-three guy. One more and we were out of the inning. But the base runner moved to second on a passed ball. And on the next pitch, the hitter bounced a seeing-eye grounder up the middle. They hadn't hit one ball hard, but Carlmont led 1–0.

Bad enough. But then Russell threw a curveball that hung over the heart of the plate. Carlmont's hitter pounded it to deep left. I kept waiting for the ball to come down, but when it finally did it was over the fence. Just like that we were down 3–0.

The score stayed 3–0 through the second and third innings. By the time Jimmy came to the plate to lead off the fourth, all sorts of crazy thoughts were running through my head. What if we didn't win? Not just that game, but any game all year. What if we were total flops, the laughingstocks of the league?

Carlmont's pitcher teased Jimmy with two slow curves that broke low and outside. But Jimmy laid off, and with the count 2-0 he was in the driver's seat. The pitcher wound, delivered — an aimed job that Jimmy laced into right center for a double.

That hit brought us to our feet on the bench. As Todd stepped to the plate, I saw him exchange a look with Jimmy. It was the same look I'd seen them exchange at the batting cage at Tom Wells. Carlmont's pitcher stretched, looked back at Jimmy, fired. Crack! The ball rose high against the sky. The left fielder took a couple of steps back, turned, and watched it disappear over the fence. Jimmy raised his hand in triumph and danced home. Todd kept his head down as he circled the bases, but he was beaming when he high-fived everybody on the bench.

146

It was only the first game, but those two hits probably saved our season. Our backs were to the wall, and both our big sticks had come through. That gave the rest of us confidence. We scored two more runs that inning on two walks and two hits to take a 4–3 lead.

Russell shut Carlmont down in their half of the fourth, and we broke it open in the fifth. I popped up, but Jimmy stroked a double to left. Carlmont's pitcher wanted nothing to do with Todd and walked him on four pitches. But with two on base, he had to come in to Fred Pacheco, and Freddie drove the second pitch he saw into left center for a two-run double. Our DH, Junior Tupo, ripped a single up the middle to bring Pacheco home. DeRego popped up to short right. It should have been the second out, but the Carlmont guys collided. Tupo scored, and DeRego ended up at third. Hill's ground out brought home the fifth run of the inning. We ended up winning 10–3. The last out came on a little two-hopper to me.

I didn't have a hit or make any great plays. But I was on the field shaking hands with the guys after the last out, and that was plenty exciting.

On the bus home, Jimmy and I rehashed the game. Then, just before we reached Woodside High, he looked out the window. "I've been thinking of calling my father," he said. "Maybe asking him to come see a game." He turned to me. "What do you think?"

"Sounds like a good idea," I answered. "He'd show if you asked him."

Jimmy nodded. "Maybe I will."

"You should," I said. "Really."

He leaned back, closed his eyes. "I can't figure

147

myself sometimes, Seth. When my father is around, I wish he would go away. But when I don't see him . . ." He stopped. "Oh, I don't know."

2♦

With that first victory under our belts, a calm settled over the team. We were all business during practice. We knew we had a chance to be good — real good.

One odd thing did happen, though. During the two-mile run, Jimmy started off running stride for stride with Sharront. But at the half-mile mark he faded, and on both Monday and Tuesday he finished in last place, his fingers under his ribs.

I wasn't used to seeing Jimmy come in last in anything. "Are you sick or something?" I asked him Tuesday.

He waved me off. "I'm sick of running, that's all."

You need two good starters and one solid reliever to go anywhere in high-school ball. Cory Russell could pitch; Mike Radinsky could close games out. The big question was Alex Furmin.

Alex was a sophomore. On the freshman team he'd been fast but wild. Being a little wild is okay. That wildness makes hitters hate to stand in. But if a pitcher can't get the ball over, the hitters take until the pitcher walks them or grooves a fastball.

Our second game was at home against Serra. It was a

148

perfect day, not hot and not cold. But during warm-ups Furmin was sweating like a pig. Somebody should have talked to him the way Jimmy had talked to me, but nobody did.

Serra's leadoff hitter took two fastballs outside, then nailed the third to deep right center. Todd ate up ground and dived at the last second. The ball caught in the webbing. He did a double roll, then held up his glove for the umpire to see.

You almost never see a great catch on the first play of the game. Fielders just aren't completely ready. But Todd's play was up there with the greatest catches I've ever seen.

I figured Todd's play would settle Furmin, but the next guy hit a shot to third. The ball would have taken Hill's head off if he hadn't caught it. The third out came on a hot smash to Jimmy. In the book it was a one-two-three inning, but Furmin hadn't fooled anyone.

Serra's pitcher was Joey Garibaldi. He'd played with Jimmy on Belmont's Babe Ruth team. "Sit on the fastball," Jimmy told us. "He can't get his curve over."

It was good advice, only Jimmy forgot to mention that Garibaldi had a live fastball. He sawed off Maxwell's bat with a hummer that Maxwell dribbled down to second for the first out. But he came in with a hanging curve to me, and I banged that pitch up the middle for my first hit of the season.

Garibaldi went back to his fastball against Jimmy, and Jimmy fouled the first two off. With an 0-2 count, Garibaldi should have wasted a pitch. But he came back with a third straight fastball. What a mistake! Jimmy ripped a drive to left that cleared the fence by twenty feet.

Sometimes a lead settles a pitcher down, but Alex was still awful in the second. Serra's leadoff hitter roped a single to left field. The next hitter flied out to deep center, but the batter after lined a single to right. Alex walked the next guy on four pitches to load the bases.

Sharront came out. "Throw the ball just like in practice," Sharront said. Alex nodded his head about thirty times. But his first pitch to the next batter had nothing on it, and the Serra guy blistered a ground single to center to drive in two runs and tie the score.

When Alex saw Radinsky starting to throw in the bullpen, he completely fell apart. He plunked the next guy in the back to reload the bases, then gave up a double that cleared them. By the time Radinsky got the call, we were down 6–2.

But we didn't quit. Jimmy nailed a single in the fourth and Todd cashed him in with a triple. Todd scored on Pacheco's single. In the sixth Maxwell doubled. I moved him to third with a ground out, and he scored on Jimmy's sacrifice fly to left. That made it 6–5, but we had only one more at bat.

"Hold them," Sharront called to Radinsky as he took the mound in the top of the seventh.

Radinsky nodded, then gave up a single to Serra's leadoff hitter. The next batter laid down a sacrifice bunt, moving the runner into scoring position. Radinsky got a pop-up for the second out, but the batter after that ripped a liner into center field for a single.

The base runner was off on contact, but so was Todd. He fielded the ball on one bounce and fired a bullet to home. That ball never was more than six feet from the ground. Johnson caught it, spun around, and put the tag down. "You're out of there!" the ump yelled.

That play pumped us as we came in for our last at bat. But the bottom of our lineup was due up, and not one of those guys had managed a hit.

DeRego drove a loud foul to left, but struck out on a slow curve. Dan Hill fought off a couple of curves and ended up bouncing a single to center. A good at bat. Lance Johnson took a rip at a fastball and belted a long drive to left. While the ball was in the air, we were shouting our heads off, because it looked like it had a chance to get out of the park, or at least go for extra bases. But Serra's left fielder stuck up his glove and got an ice-cream cone. Two out.

I moved to the on-deck circle as Maxwell strode to the plate. Talk about your guts churning. I was afraid Maxwell would make an out and we'd lose. I was afraid he'd get a hit and the game would be on my shoulders. I was afraid Sharront would yank me and send up a pinch hitter. I was afraid he wouldn't yank me and I'd strike out.

Maxwell worked the count full. Then he hit a flare to short right. I didn't breathe as I watched the right fielder close on the ball, dive . . . and have it skip off his glove. Maxwell took second when the ball dribbled off into foul territory, and Hill moved to third.

I looked down to Sharront. Was he going to pull me? He clapped his hands. "All right, Seth, a little bingo."

151

I took a couple of vicious practice swings, then stepped in. I figured the pitcher would figure I was taking all the way. So I decided if I got a fastball, I'd hack at it.

And I got it — a fastball belt-high on the outside corner. I swung level, rolling my hands over. I didn't pound the ball, but I caught it solid. As I took the first steps out of the box, I watched the second baseman jump. For a second I thought he'd snare it, but the ball cleared his glove by six inches, a clean single. Hill trotted in with the tying run. The right fielder tried to make a play on Maxwell, but Devon had the afterburners going, and he slid in safely. We'd won, 7–6.

The guys surrounded me, pounding me on the back and shaking my hand so hard my shoulder hurt. We whooped it up all the way into the shower room.

When the noise quieted down, Jimmy pulled me aside. "Some of the guys are planning a victory celebration tonight at Huddart Park."

"Sounds good," I said as I dried myself off. "Sounds real good."

And it did sound good. I felt like celebrating — like lying back, looking up at the stars, and drinking a few beers with the guys. It wasn't until after dinner that I thought it through.

It was a crazy risk. Crazy for Jimmy. If he got caught, it would be the second strike against him. One more screwup after that and Sharront would kick him off the team. Not exactly the way to impress major-league scouts.

And crazy for me. If I got caught, I'd be suspended from the team. Sharront would give second base to

152

Duncan and stick me on the bench. And there was something else, too. I'd given my word to my mother; I'd made a promise to myself.

After dinner I phoned Jimmy. "Listen," I told him. "Let's skip Huddart Park. We can catch a movie instead."

There was a long pause. "I don't feel much like a movie," Jimmy finally said.

"You could come over here. The Braves are on the tube."

Another long pause. "I think I'll just stay in, Seth. Maybe go to bed early. I'm pretty tired."

I hung up, but I felt restless all evening. I couldn't watch the game; I couldn't do schoolwork. I took a shower, and with the water pouring over my head I found myself thinking all sorts of crazy thoughts. There were too many things I wasn't sure about.

When I came out of the bathroom, my mother was at the kitchen table reading the newspaper. I went out to kiss her good night, but instead of going back to my bedroom I sat down across from her. I figured I could maybe get one thing cleared up.

She put the newspaper aside. "Something bothering you, Seth?"

"Not really," I answered, chickening out.

She folded her hands in front of her. "Something is on your mind. What is it?"

"Well," I said, looking away, "I was just wondering if, well, if you think you'll ever get married again."

My mother laughed, a quick, embarrassed laugh. "What brings this up?"

153

"I don't know," I answered. "It's just something that came to me while I was in the shower. You don't have to answer if you don't want. It's no big deal."

She opened her hands, put them flat on the table. "No, it's a fair question, so I'll answer. Yes, Seth, if the right man comes along I will remarry, but I promise you it will not be until after you've moved out of the house."

I thought about that for a second. "Why not sooner?"

"I don't know. Just a sense I have, a sense that it would be better for you if I waited." She stopped. "Am I wrong?"

"No. You're not wrong."

She nodded. "I didn't think I was." The clock ticked on the wall. "Anything else on your mind?"

I shook my head. "No, nothing."

She stood, kissed me on the forehead. "Good, because I'm going to bed."

She opened the kitchen door, but before she went down the hall I called her back. "Mother."

"What is it, Seth?"

"Thank you."

She smiled, a smile I'll never forget.

"You're welcome."

3♦

Russell was sharp on Sunday against Palo Alto. Jimmy and Todd both went three for four. Todd had a homer and Jimmy had two more doubles. Both made great plays in the field. Todd snagged a sinking liner in the third; in the sixth Jimmy fielded a shot deep in the hole and fired across the diamond in time. I banged out two hits and scored twice — but it seemed like everybody scored twice. We crushed them 14–2.

That game Jimmy and I turned our first double plays of the season. The first came in the second inning when the game was still close. Palo Alto had runners on the corners with one out. The ball was a sharp grounder to Jimmy's right. He speared it, turned, fired the ball to me. I unloaded quickly and doubled up the runner. That was a pretty one, and it took some air out of Palo Alto.

The second didn't matter so much. We were up 13–2 in the sixth. They had a runner on first, and the batter smacked a one-hopper right to me. Once I'd fielded it, the double play was automatic. Still, it felt good to see 4-6-3 in the score book when the game was over.

At 3-0, we were off to a great start. But there was still the problem of the second starter. Sharront spent all of Tuesday's practice going over mechanics with Alex: leg kick, release point, follow-through.

In the locker room after practice, Alex looked tight. "It'll be okay, Alex," I said to him as I headed to the shower. "It'll be okay." He gave me a weak smile. Todd stopped and said something to Alex, too. And when I came out of the shower, I saw Jimmy with him. We all knew how much was riding on his left arm.

At school Wednesday I was hoping to see Alex so I could give him a good word. I hated to think of him working himself into a total state like he'd done before. But I didn't see him — or Jimmy either — until we were actually on the field warming up for the game, and

155

then I didn't like what I saw. Alex wasn't jumpy, but his face was green, and he had bags under his eyes.

We started fast. Maxwell singled up the middle. I laid down a bunt to move him to second. Jimmy lined out to center, but Todd ripped a double to bring Maxwell home. When Mitty's pitcher uncorked a wild pitch, Todd took third, and he scored when the second baseman booted Pacheco's grounder.

Alex looked sick, but his fastball was wicked. He struck out the leadoff batter on three pitches, then hit the next guy in the thigh. "Keep humming them in there," Jimmy called in. That's what Alex did. The number-three and number-four hitters both went down swinging at fastballs.

We pecked away at Mitty, scoring again in the third, and putting up two more in the fourth. Alex stayed fast and wild, throwing a million pitches, striking out a slew of guys, and walking a slew of guys. That kind of pitching is murder on fielders. It's hard to keep on your toes. I made my first error in the fourth, and Jimmy had one too.

Still, at the end of five innings we were up 6–0. Alex had ten strikeouts but was totally exhausted. Sharront lifted him and brought in Alan Willis.

Willis is a good guy, but he doesn't have much stuff. Mitty scored twice in the sixth, and once more in the seventh. They even brought the tying run to the plate before Sharront called on Radinsky to close it out.

After the game we all crowded around Alex's locker, telling him how great he'd done. He was happy, but somehow not as happy as he should have been.

"Are you all right?" I asked.

"Yeah, yeah, I'm fine," he answered.

As we moved back toward our own lockers, Todd turned to me. "You know what's wrong with him?"

"No," I answered. "What?"

"He's hung over. So is your friend Jimmy."

"What are you talking about?" I said.

"Jimmy's found some hole-in-the-wall grocery where he can buy beer. He's been hounding guys to go drinking with him."

I was confused. "And you never go, I suppose."

Todd looked at me like I was out of my mind. "Are you crazy? After last year? Maybe I'm not as bright as you, Seth, but I'm not stupid."

I opened my locker, pulled out my clothes. Todd stayed right with me.

"So why are you telling me all this?" I asked him.

He shrugged. "I'm telling you because you're Jimmy's best friend. Unless somebody does something, he's going to get himself kicked off the team. And he's going to take other guys with him. Good-bye league championship. Good-bye state tournament. Good-bye everything we're working for."

"What do you want me to do?"

"Talk to him," Todd said. "He might listen to you."

That night I thought long and hard about what Todd had said. For a while I was mad at him. He was the guy who had gotten Jimmy started with drinking. In a way the whole thing was his fault, and he was trying to dump it all on me. It wasn't fair.

157

Then I considered dumping it onto somebody else. Adults are always saying you should report stuff like drinking for the good of your friends, so they can get help. But I knew all along I wouldn't report Jimmy. Sharront would suspend him. Another mistake and Jimmy would get booted off the team. Big help that would be.

Todd was right — it was up to me to talk sense to Jimmy. But I couldn't just call him up and say, "Hey, Jimmy, stop acting like a fool." I had to pick the right place and the right time.

4♦

Finding the right place and time wasn't easy. I was up at six every morning. I'd finish my homework, polish off a couple bowls of cereal, and leave for school by seven. My first class was at seven-thirty. The school day flew by. Chemistry, English, history, gym, lunch, French, study hall.

I suppose I could have talked to Jimmy after practice or called him at night, but I didn't do it. Twice during the next week Todd asked me if I'd done anything, and both times I had to shake my head.

"It's going to explode in his face," Todd said the second time. "I'm telling you — right in his face."

That week we had games against Cupertino and Santa Cruz. We won 12–0 and 11–3. Neither team could field, and their pitchers kept coming in with fat pitches. Jimmy had a season in those two games: seven hits, two of them home runs and three of them doubles. Maybe that's an-

other reason I didn't say anything. When a guy is hitting
.550, it's tough to tell him he's screwing up the team.
Jimmy wasn't the only guy going well. Russell
pitched a shutout on Wednesday, and Alex — calmer
with each victory — struck out eight in five innings on
Sunday. I went three for nine. The only player who
slumped was Todd. He went zero for eight, with four
strikeouts.

During Monday's practice the ball was jumping off
our bats, and guys were making circus catches in the
field. We were winning and loose and happy, or least
that's how it seemed.

At the end of practice Sharront blew the whistle and
we hit the track for the two-mile run. As usual, Sharront
took the early lead. Jimmy didn't challenge him, not
even for a lap. But Todd ran right at Sharront's shoulder.

Todd's face was grim; his eyes determined. It was as
if he were trying to run out all the frustration of his batting slump. In the last hundred yards he turned it on, and
he beat Sharront by ten yards.

In the locker room afterward guys were congratulating
Todd, giving him high-fives. He didn't even crack a
smile. Instead, he strode over to Jimmy's locker.
"Where were you, Winter?" he demanded.

"What are you talking about?" Jimmy asked.

"During the race. Where were you?"

Jimmy closed his locker. "I didn't have it today.
That's all. Today was your day."

"How come you didn't have it?"

Jimmy pulled on his socks. "I just didn't have it.
What's it to you?"

"Are you hung over, Winter?" Todd asked. "Is that why you couldn't run?"

Jimmy turned bright red. "Who are you? My mom? Mind your own business."

"If it affects the team it's my business. You're going to blow everything for everybody."

Jimmy stood, stared him in the eye. "I'll tell you who's going to blow everything. You. And you know why? Because you can't hit anymore. You're a choker."

Immediately Todd took a swing at Jimmy, catching him on the top of the head and knocking him back over the bench. Jimmy scrambled to his feet, ready to mix it up, but Pacheco and Johnson pulled them apart.

5♦

That settled it. There was no more sitting on the fence — I had to do something. After dinner I picked up the phone and started to punch in Jimmy's number. Halfway through I stopped. Some things you can't talk about over the phone.

When I rang the doorbell, Jimmy's mother answered. "He's in his room," she said.

I found him sitting on the floor, his baseball cards in front of him, like he was a little kid. "Hey, Seth. What's up?"

"Nothing much," I answered. "I thought maybe you'd want to go get a pizza or something."

"Sure. Why not?"

He slowly gathered up his cards, put them carefully away. Then we drove over to Round Table on the El
160

Camino. "So what's the deal," Jimmy said once we'd bought our food.

I beat around the bush. "The team is never going to win with you and Todd fighting."

He gave me a half-smile. "What are you talking about? Lots of teams have guys who don't get along, and they win. I don't have to tell you that. You've read every baseball book there is."

We ate in silence for a while. Then I came out with it. "Or if you get kicked off the team for drinking."

He leaned back in his chair. "So that's it." He shook his head. "Okay, I have a few beers sometimes. Big deal. Half the kids in the school drink. If I remember correctly, you used to be one of them."

I felt like a hypocrite, but I plunged forward. "So I used to drink. So what? It was stupid then, and it's stupid to keep being stupid."

Jimmy bent his straw back and forth a few times. "Seth, do me a favor. Take care of yourself, take care of second base. And I promise you I'll take care of myself, and I'll take care of shortstop. Is that a deal?"

I'd gone too far to back down. "No, it's not a deal." I paused. "Look," I said, "you've got to —"

Jimmy stood, leaned forward across the table so that his face was right in mine. "Seth, mind your own business. Okay? Mind your own business."

6♦

Tuesday Todd's hand was so swollen he couldn't throw or hit.

"What happened?" Sharront asked.

"I was helping my dad unload bricks," Todd explained, "and one of them dropped."

That raised Sharront's eyebrows. "My hand once was swollen like that. But it was from a fistfight."

Todd kept his cool. "I wasn't in a fight. I dropped a brick on it. You can call my dad."

Wednesday afternoon we were on the road against Sequoia. Todd's hand was still swollen. He wanted to play, but Sharront wouldn't go along. "Let it heal. It's a long season. Bill McDonald will play center."

Sequoia's pitcher was like Furmin — fast and wild. In the first Maxwell walked to lead off, and then he stole second. I struck out, but Jimmy singled him home. Pacheco walked, and then McDonald walked to load the bases. One more hit would have broken the game open. But DeRego and Hill both popped up.

That's how the game went for us — lots of runners, but not many runs. We scored again in the third, and then Jimmy hit one out of the ballpark to lead off the sixth. It was an incredible home run; if the ball hadn't hit a eucalyptus tree it would have landed on the El Camino. Heading to the bottom of the seventh we led 3–0. Russell had given up only two hits and one walk, but Sharront wasn't taking any chances. He had Radinsky warming up in the bullpen.

Sequoia's leadoff hitter took a weird little half-swing on Russell's first pitch. The ball kind of knuckled out toward short right. I dived and had the ball in the leather of my glove — but when I hit the ground, it popped loose.

162

I walked the ball in to Russell, feeling pretty down.

"Forget it, Seth," he said.

The next batter bounced a seeing-eye single right up the middle. That brought the tying run to the plate.

Russell took off his cap, ran his hand through his hair, and put his cap back on. Then he stretched, looked the runners back, delivered. The bat flashed, and the ball rocketed down the line into the left-field corner. By the time Pacheco fired it back to the infield, two runs were in, and the tying runner was standing at third.

Sharront brought in Radinsky. We played the infield in trying to cut off the run at the plate. Radinsky struck out the first guy he faced, but then walked the next batter on a 3-2 fastball that I swear was a strike. Runners were at the corners with only one out.

Sharront had Jimmy and me move back to double-play depth. That was great, feeling his confidence in us. *Hit it to me,* I thought. *Or hit it to Jimmy.* I wanted to prove to Sharront that he was right, that we could turn two in the clutch.

But instead of hitting a grounder, Sequoia's hitter smacked a line drive to straightaway center. That's the hardest ball to judge — one hit right at you. McDonald took one fatal step back, then charged. At the last second he dived, trying for a shoestring catch. For an instant I thought he'd done it. But then I saw the ball rolling out toward the center-field fence. By the time Pacheco ran the ball down, the tying and winning runs had crossed the plate. The Sequoia guys were going crazy, and our heads were hanging.

It's only four miles from Sequoia to Woodside, but

163

that bus ride took forever. McDonald sat alone. He was blaming himself, but nobody else was blaming him.

If Todd hadn't taken a swing at Jimmy, he would have been in center field. And he would have caught that line drive. Every guy on the team knew it. "Mind your own business." That's what Jimmy had told me to do. Maybe he was right.

7♦

The first St. Francis game was at home on Sunday afternoon. They were undefeated, so a loss would drop us two back and just about end our chances for the league title and the state tournament berth that went with it.

Alex was starting for us, and he had his good stuff. The St. Francis guys were flinching, stepping in the bucket, striking out. Every once in a while Alex would uncork a wild pitch, and that really unnerved them.

Randy Morris pitched for St. Francis. Curveball, change-up, change-up, curveball, fastball, fastball. No pattern, no two pitches the same speed. The first time up I lunged at a curve and grounded to first. The next time around I was way out in front of a change-up and struck out.

I wasn't the only guy having trouble. Even Jimmy looked bad, grounding out softly in his first two at bats. Todd had a single in the second, and Lance Johnson got another in the third. But after six innings those two hits were all we had.

But they were two more hits than St. Francis had.

When Alex came out to start the seventh, he was working on a no-hitter. He was also dead tired. After he finished his warm-ups, he leaned forward, his hands on his knees — a sure sign of exhaustion.

St. Francis's leadoff hitter took the first two pitches for balls. He stepped out, looked down the third-base line for a sign. With a 2-0 count late in a scoreless game, it's automatic to take. At least that's what I thought. I'm sure it's what Alex thought too, because he grooved a fastball right down the middle.

The guy swung away. And did he ever hit it! A bolt down the left-field line. There was never any doubt about the distance, but I kept thinking it was going to curve foul, that it *had* to curve foul.

After it cleared the fence, the umpire stared long and hard, then raised his right hand, pointed his finger in the air, and rotated his wrist — the signal for a home run.

Everyone was stunned. In a pitchers' duel it sometimes seems as though no one will ever score. So to have it happen — bang — was like walking into a swinging door.

Sharront hooked Alex. Radinsky retired the next three batters on ground outs. I ran to the dugout, slumped onto the bench. I'll admit I thought our chances were down the tubes. We hadn't been able to touch Morris, and warming up behind him was Steve Cannon.

Then Jimmy stood, his green eyes on fire. He looked up and down the bench. ''Don't quit!'' he said to everyone and no one. ''If you get me to the plate, I'll win this game for you. I promise.''

165

It was an incredible thing to say. Had anybody else said it, I would have thought he was making a fool of himself. But I believed in Jimmy. We all did. It wasn't just talk. If Jimmy got the chance, he'd deliver.

But that was a big if. Jimmy was batting fifth that inning. We'd need two base runners to bring him up.

The inning started well. Dan Hill looped a dying quail into short right. Without hesitating, he flew around first and went into second headfirst. The throw was off-line — we had the tying run in scoring position.

St. Francis's coach walked slowly to the mound. There was never any doubt. They'd made Steve Cannon a reliever for exactly this situation.

What a pitcher!

My stomach knotted as I watched Cannon warm up. He seemed bigger and stronger and faster than ever. And what style! He did everything slow. He rubbed the ball up slow; he got the sign from the catcher slow; he tied his shoes slow. Then he'd go into his motion, and the ball would explode out of his hand.

Sharront wanted Johnson to bunt Hill to third. From there Hill could score on a ground out, a sac fly, a wild pitch, a passed ball. Good strategy, but Cannon ruined it by burning three hard fastballs right by Johnson for the first out.

Maxwell stepped into the batter's box, and I moved to the on-deck circle. Maxwell choked up on the bat, but it didn't do him any good. Cannon blew two strikes by him, wasted a curve inside, then struck him out with another untouchable fastball. Two outs.

166

I started toward the plate, feeling like I was going to my execution, when Jimmy grabbed my elbow. His fingers dug so deeply into my flesh it hurt. "Get on base, Seth," he said, his eyes boring into me.

"I'll try, Jimmy," I whispered.

"Don't try," he answered. "Do it!"

I stood way back in the batter's box, so far back I could barely reach the outside corner of the plate. I told myself standing deep would give me more time to catch up with Cannon's fastball. But the true reason was fear.

Cannon looked like an animal out on the mound. His hair was matted down, and his eyes were as wild as Jimmy's. Cannon stretched, checked the runner at second, came in. Fastball, right down the pike, belt-high. I swung, level and smooth, and caught nothing but air.

I stepped out.

"Get a hit!" Jimmy screamed at me. The guys on the bench were screaming the same thing. Our chances for the league championship, the state tournament were riding on my at bat.

My head was pounding. I felt like turning on everyone, screaming back at them. "But I can't do it. Don't you understand? I'm not good enough."

I adjusted my helmet, stepped back in. Cannon went into his stretch, then blew another fastball by me for strike two.

Right then, when everything seemed completely hopeless, an idea came to me. It was a long shot, but it was my only shot. At 0-2 Cannon might waste a curveball inside. I inched closer to the plate.

Cannon delivered. And then it was there, right on me. Only not a curve, but a fastball six inches inside.

It's one thing to think about taking one for the team, but as that ball was bearing down on me like a train, every nerve in my body screamed that I should jump back. I willed myself to hang in there. I willed it. I took that fastball square in the back. The pain roared up my spine and filled my brain, driving me to my knees. I don't know what it feels like to be shot, but it can't feel a whole lot worse than being hit by a ninety-mile-an-hour fastball.

"Take your base!" the umpire yelled.

As I started to get up, I felt Sharront's hand on my shoulder. "Take a few deep breaths."

I didn't argue. I felt like my body was stuck in a vise that somebody was tightening little by little.

When I finally stood, Sharront sent Duncan in to run for me. "Way to go," he whispered as he led me back to the bench. "Way to go."

I'm not a nail biter, but as I sat on the bench fighting the pain, I bit them.

Jimmy Winter vs. Steve Cannon; power vs. power.

Cannon's first pitch was a fastball down the heart of the plate. Jimmy uncoiled, but missed it. Strike one. The park quieted as Cannon walked around the mound a little. The noise slowly built as he returned to the rubber. He stretched, came in with another fastball. This time Jimmy caught a piece of it and sent a foul back into the screen.

Jimmy stepped out. He rubbed some dirt into his batting gloves while Cannon rubbed up the ball. The noise built again, louder than before.

Cannon won't be able to blow another one past Jimmy, I remember thinking. *Jimmy's going to nail this one.*

Cannon toed the rubber, stretched. No waste pitch this time. Just another fastball down the heart. Jimmy drove through the ball with his legs. And he caught it solid, a rifle shot to right center. The ball landed between the outfielders and rolled all the way to the fence. Hill scored easily. With two outs, Duncan was off on contact. We were going crazy on the bench, jumping up and down as he raced around the bases. Their center fielder hit the relay man, but the throw home was way up the line. Duncan scored the winning run standing up.

We mobbed Jimmy at second base. You'd have thought we'd won the title right then and there the way we acted. We lifted him on our shoulders and carried him off the field. We were hollering so much and so long in the shower room that Sharront finally came in, blew his whistle. "This was one game," he shouted. "Don't forget it."

We quieted, but in our hearts we felt that we were on our way, that nothing could stop us.

Jimmy came over. "How's your back?"

I'd forgotten about it. I looked down and saw a huge black bruise. "It hurts," I said, smiling.

Jimmy put both of his hands on my shoulders and looked me in the eye. "That took more guts than I've got, Seth."

169

8♦

The next morning I kept looking for Jimmy at school. I don't know what I wanted to say exactly. Maybe I didn't want to say anything. Maybe all I wanted was to be near him, to feed off his magic. Because on the diamond that's what he was — magic.

I looked around for him before school and during lunch, but I never tracked him down. In fact I didn't see him until I was in the locker room dressing for practice. He was surrounded by Alex Furmin, Dan Hill, and those guys. They were joking around, like everybody. We were all feeling pretty loosey-goosey.

Then Sharront stuck his head in. "Jimmy Winter," he shouted, "to my office."

"What's it about?" a couple of guys asked Jimmy as he wound his way through the locker room.

Jimmy shrugged. "Beats me."

I got a sick feeling as I watched Jimmy disappear into the office, and I wasn't the only one. The place turned into a morgue. I finished dressing, trudged out to the field, and played some catch with Alan Willis. Finally Sharront came out — without Jimmy.

"Gentlemen," he said, his face grim. "Jimmy Winter has been suspended from the team. He seems to have forgotten that to play on a school team, you have to attend school. So let me remind all of you. Family first . . . school second . . . baseball third." He clapped his hands. "Now let's get going. I want a good practice today!"

You get it in your head that one thing is the problem, and you forget about everything else. I'd been worried

170

that drinking would bring Jimmy down. Cutting classes — I didn't have a clue he was doing that.

Sharront put Duncan at second and moved me to shortstop. I felt all wrong there. It was Jimmy's spot, not mine. The throw from the hole seemed miles long. I one-hopped most of them over to DeRego. "You're not at second base, Barham," Sharront kept hollering. "You can't arm the ball over to first. Plant your back foot and throw."

As I walked home, my mind was on Jimmy, not on baseball. Everything was there for him, just waiting for him to reach out and grab it. So why was he acting so stupid?

As I turned up the walkway to my house, Jimmy popped out at me from behind a tree. "Hey, Seth, you got a minute?"

"Yeah, sure," I answered, getting hold of myself. "Just let me check with my mother."

"It's dinnertime, Seth," she said.

"Mom, it's important."

She frowned. "Okay. Only make it quick."

I shook my head. "It might not be quick."

"All right," she answered. "I'll put your plate in the oven."

Jimmy and I walked over to Henry Ford and sat on the swings. "What's going on, Jimmy?" I asked. "Why are you doing this to yourself?"

He looked annoyed. "Seth, what have I done that's so awful? Sometimes I wake up and I don't feel like facing history and English and math. So I go to Tom Wells, hit some balls, hang out until it's time for

171

baseball practice. Where's the big crime?''

I thought for a while. "No big crime, Jimmy," I said. "But you've got to pass your classes to play. That's how it works.''

"School is stupid," he said.

I shrugged. "You've got to do it.''

"Yeah, yeah," he said. "I've heard it a million times.''

We sat for a couple of minutes. "Look," he finally said, "I need a favor.''

"Sure. What is it?''

"I'm supposed to write a term paper on Turkey for history class. Those papers kill me, but I bet you could whip something out pretty fast.''

I felt almost sick. "Jimmy, I'll help you if you want. But I won't write it for you.''

"Why not? It doesn't have to be good. Actually it would be better if it was lousy. If it's too good Ms. Leila would suspect.''

"I don't want to cheat.''

"Oh, come off it, Seth. It's not like I'm headed to Stanford or applying for a job at the UN. All I want to do is play ball.'' He picked up a rock, tossed it. "Do I have to beg?''

I took a deep breath. "Okay, I'll do it. I don't want to, but I'll do it.''

We walked back then, Jimmy to his house and me to mine. Neither of us said a word as we parted. When I opened my front door, the last thing I wanted was another argument. But that's what I got.

"So," my mother said, "what was that about?''

172

"Nothing," I answered.

"No, Seth. It's not about nothing. I want to hear what's going on."

I flopped down on the sofa. I left out the stuff about writing his paper, but I told her everything else about Jimmy's suspension. "It's not fair," I said when I finished.

"What else could the coach have done?" she asked.

"Oh, I don't know." I thought for a second. "Why should Jimmy have to go to school? He's going to be a major leaguer. He'll make millions. Why can't he just play ball?"

"Seth, I don't know why our world is the way it is," she said, "and I'm not going to pretend I do. Driving to work, I look at all the people in their cars. Most of them don't want to be going where they're going. I sure don't want to be. I don't know why we can't all do exactly what we want to do. But the world doesn't work that way."

She frowned. "And there's something else, too. Something that you know and I know, though you've been trying to keep it from me, and maybe from yourself. Your friend isn't some sort of Peter Pan who just wants to play in the park all day. Jimmy's got a drug problem or a drinking problem, or both."

"You don't know that," I snapped.

She folded her arms across her chest. "I can't prove it, Seth. But I know it. And you know it, too."

I did my homework, took a shower, and went to bed. But it took me so long to fall asleep that I was exhausted

173

the next morning. So when I saw Jimmy in the library before school, I tried to dodge him. I didn't feel like talking to anybody. But he spotted me, motioned me over.

"Seth, forget about what I asked you to do yesterday."

"You mean the paper?" I said, not sure I understood.

"Yeah."

I was startled. "Are you sure?"

"Yeah, I'm sure."

"I'll help if you want."

The bell rang. "I can do it myself," Jimmy said as he gathered his books for class. "You think I'm stupid, but I'm not."

I could tell he was angry. I hadn't meant to humiliate him, but I guess I had. I didn't care though. The important thing was that he was taking school as a challenge, and I'd never known Jimmy to back down from a challenge. *Everything is going to be okay,* I told myself as I went off to my class. *Everything is going to work out just fine.*

9♦

I sweated bullets before our next game. The whole team did. We were all wondering how we'd play without Jimmy. We knew we could survive a few games without his bat and his glove; we didn't know if we could win without his heart.

But we caught a break. Actually we caught seven of them. That's how many errors Menlo Atherton made.

The first came on Devon Maxwell's leadoff at bat. He hit a little two-hopper toward first that their guy butchered. The ball ended up rolling off into no-man's-land down the right-field line and Maxwell scooted to third. I brought him home with a line single to left. Pacheco drew a walk, setting the table for Todd.

As I led off second base, I could feel a difference in him. He moved more slowly, seemed more sure of himself. His eyes had a ferocious look, like a guy about ready to bust loose.

Menlo Atherton's pitcher played around with a couple of curves that dipped outside, the kind of pitches Todd had been swinging at for weeks. But he let them both go.

Count — that's the name of the game for all hitters. At 0-2 the pitcher has you at his mercy. But at 2-0 Todd dug in, looking for his pitch. And he got it. He lined a bullet to the fence in left center. I scored standing, and Pacheco came in right behind me. By the time the first was over, we were up 5–0.

We ended up winning 13–4. Todd went four for five, with two more doubles. Even the time he made an out he smoked the ball, a line shot right at the shortstop.

Todd kept hitting the ball. He had three hits in our victory over San Carlos, and he launched a three-run homer in the sixth to lead us past Sunnyvale.

That night Jimmy called me. "You're moving tomorrow," he said, and I could tell he was in high spirits.

"What are you talking about?"

"To second base."

It clicked in. "Are you eligible?"

"I got a seventy-eight on my math makeup. Ms. Leila said my paper on Turkey was a little rough, but she gave me a C." He paused. "I'm back on the team, Seth. And I'm not going to be off it again."

10♦

Sharront didn't horse around like some coaches do, pretending that Jimmy would have to win his spot back. "You're batting third and playing shortstop," he said when Jimmy came out on the field. Then Sharront patted him on the butt. "Your teachers report you've done good work. We're glad to have you back."

Jimmy smiled. "I'm glad to be back."

I watched Todd all during practice, hoping he'd say something to Jimmy. He didn't, and that had me down a bit. But just before the two-mile run, Jimmy went over to Todd.

I didn't hear what they said, but I do know they shook hands at the end. The two of them ran side by side the entire race and finished that way, tied for first, about twenty yards ahead of Sharront.

In the locker room Jimmy was full of the future. "I've got it together now, Seth, I really do. No more garbage. Just baseball."

It was as if all the pieces to some giant jigsaw puzzle suddenly had fallen together perfectly. I could feel the league title — maybe even the state title — coming our way.

* * *

What a run we had! Maxwell was getting on, stealing bases. I was moving him up, dropping in a hit here and there. And Jimmy and Todd were knocking out extra-base hits like they were hamburgers from McDonald's. Pacheco's average was down around .200, but when he hit the ball it was for extra bases. Tupo, DeRego, Hill, Johnson — it seemed like every game at least one of those guys came up with something big.

Our fielding was super, too. We were wound tight, not in a bad way that causes errors, but like tigers getting ready to spring. Everybody on the team had a hunger to get to the ball. We made one error in four games — a good stat for a major-league team, amazing for a high-school team.

Jimmy was an acrobat at short. Nothing was getting by him. They talk about players moving with the crack of the bat. Jimmy moved before the crack of the bat. Somehow he could tell whether the guy was out in front of a pitch or whether he was swinging late. The ground he covered was unbelievable.

The scorecard read "6-4-3" more than a few times. They call the double play the pitcher's best friend. Russell and Furmin had a lot of best friends all through that streak. We pounded Carlmont, 8–1; Serra, 11–2; Mitty, 7–0; Palo Alto, 9–4; Cupertino, 13–1. It would have been total heaven if it weren't for one thing — St. Francis matched us win for win.

Coaches tell you to play your own game and not worry about the competition. Easy to say; not so easy to do. When I got home after a game, I'd call the *Tribune* and ask the guy at the sports desk how St. Francis had done.

177

The first time I was real sheepish, afraid he'd want to know who I was and why I cared. But he didn't. He did grumble though. "We're thinking about putting in a special number, a high-school-sports hot line," he told me. "You guys wear us out with these phone calls." Then he gave the score. St. Francis 5, Sequoia 4.

That's how their victories were. Close games. All of them. But the standings don't show whether your games are close or blowouts. The only thing they show is your record, and we were tied for first.

11♦

We had just hammered Saratoga 7–1. I was in the shower letting the hot water pound on my body. Sliding headfirst into second base, I'd scraped some skin off my ribs. The hot water hurt and felt good at the same time. Everybody was talking and singing and laughing around me. Then, from across the room, I heard Alex.

"Jimmy, some of us are going up to Huddart Park tonight. You feel like coming along?"

I don't know how I heard him. Twelve other guys must have been talking. But I heard him. Immediately I turned to look at Jimmy. I could feel him wanting to say *yes*. All the way across the room I could feel that.

"Not tonight, Alex," Jimmy muttered at last.

"Well, we'll be there if you change your mind," Alex answered.

As I dressed, I saw Alex and Dan Hill huddled together. I don't know for sure that they were talking about
178

partying, but they probably were. I caught Jimmy staring at them, too.

You don't decide anything important once. It would be nice if you could, but you can't. What really happens is that you have to decide again and again, every day, every hour, every minute. Nothing is ever over.

12♦

Our game Wednesday was against Sequoia, which was a break for us. We might have looked past any other team, saving ourselves up for the showdown with St. Francis on Sunday. But we couldn't look past Sequoia, not after the beating they'd laid on us the first time around.

There was a bad omen early. Alex kept stretching his shoulder as he warmed up. Then he walked the first three batters he faced. Sharront trotted out. "What's wrong?"

"My arm feels tight," he said.

Sharront pawed at the ground. "You want to come out?"

Alex shook his head. "I'll be all right."

But he wasn't. He walked the next guy on four pitches, forcing in a run. Sequoia was on the verge of breaking the game open, but their number-five hitter saved us. He swung at the first pitch. I don't know why, since Alex couldn't throw strikes. But I'm glad he did. He smacked the ball on two hops right to Jimmy. The run scored, giving them a 2–0 lead, but we turned the double play in a flash. Those two runs were all they got that inning.

179

Maxwell popped up to lead off our half of the first. But I managed a single up the middle, and Jimmy singled me to third. That brought Todd to the plate with a chance to get us right back in it.

I would have let him hit away, but Sharront put a play on. I edged off third. Sequoia's pitcher stretched. Jimmy took his lead off first. The pitcher looked over, delivered. Jimmy was off. The catcher popped up, fired the ball down to second. As soon as the ball left the catcher's hand, I raced for home.

Only the catcher hadn't thrown down to second. He'd rifled the ball back to the pitcher. A trick play — and I'd fallen for it. I was hung out to dry, halfway between third and home. I couldn't even keep the rundown going long enough for Jimmy to take third. I felt like an idiot as I trotted back to the bench.

Instead of one out with runners on the corners, we had two outs and a runner at second. Todd drove a deep fly to center. It would have scored me if I'd been on third. But it was just a long out, and Sequoia was still up by two runs.

Alex started the second inning the same way he'd started the game — throwing balls. He walked the first guy, then another guy. Sharront came out again. "I can't get loose," Alex repeated. "I just can't."

Sharront motioned for Alan Willis.

It was what I'd dreaded for a long time. Our weak spot, long relief.

After Alan took his warm-up tosses, we huddled at the mound. Willis tried to look calm, but I could feel his nerves. "Keep the ball low," Jimmy said to him. "You
180

get them to hit the ball on the ground, and Seth and me will take care of you.''

Willis nodded. Fear was in his eyes.

"You can do it, Alan," Jimmy said. He paused. "You can. Low. No matter how hard they hit the ball, if it's on the ground, Seth and me will get it.''

Willis didn't have much on the ball, but he kept it down. That meant a lot of hard ground balls to Jimmy and me. It was like taking fielding practice, only it was for real. In the fourth I snagged a hot shot up the middle, and in the fifth Jimmy made a backhand stop deep in the hole and threw the guy out by half a step.

With two out in our half of the sixth, Maxwell punched a single up the middle. Sharront clapped his hands. "Okay, Barham," he shouted, "keep it going."

Luck. If you're going to win a title, you need a little luck. The first pitch was a fastball in. I started to go, then tried to check my swing. The ball hit the handle of the bat and flared out toward short right. The second baseman didn't break on the ball at all, and the first baseman turned the wrong way, got his feet tangled up, and fell. The ball landed fair on the edge of the outfield grass, and then kicked into foul territory. By the time the outfielder ran it down, I was standing at second and Maxwell was at third.

Sequoia's coach walked out to the mound. While he talked to his pitcher, he kept looking from Jimmy to Todd, from Todd to Jimmy. Finally, he nodded and returned to the bench. The catcher held up four fingers. They were going to walk Jimmy to set up a force play at every base. But that meant they were putting the potential winning run on base — an insult to Todd.

So Todd was plenty psyched when he stepped up to the plate. The Sequoia pitcher must have figured it was a perfect spot for a change-up, but Todd was thinking the same way. He unloaded on it, smashing a long, towering grand slam way over the fence in left. Radinsky came in and closed them out. We won 4–2.

The stage was set for the showdown with St. Francis.

13♦

Those were the longest three days of my life. I kept spacing out. I'd read twenty pages in English or history and then realize I hadn't followed a word. At dinner my mother would ask a question and I'd stare at her. She'd have to ask again. I'd answer, only to drift off.

Failure. That's what consumed me. Striking out with the game on the line. Blowing a grounder, dropping a pop-up. I thought about the major leaguers who woke up one day with vertigo or some mental block — second basemen who couldn't get the ball over to first, hitters who could hit only in an empty park. Maybe something weird like that would happen to me.

I wasn't the only nervous guy. At practice I'd look at my teammates. I could feel the sourness of their stomachs in their pained faces. Todd told me he was throwing up after every meal; Alex admitted he hadn't slept in two days.

Even Jimmy was feeling it. He'd talk a good line. "Isn't this great!" he'd say. "Isn't this the best! This is

what it's all about, Seth. I can hardly wait for Sunday."
That's what he said. But when he spoke, his voice qua-
vered, and his left eye had a little twitch that grew worse
every day.

Saturday night I woke up at two in the morning. There
was a light in the kitchen. My mother was drinking tea
and eating toast. "You should be sleeping," she said
when I opened the door.

"So should you," I replied.

She stirred her tea. "I couldn't. Nerves, I guess."

I stuck some bread in the toaster, poured myself a
glass of milk, and sat down.

It was one of those times when I knew she was thinking about my father. And she knew I knew.

"Tomorrow will be a big day for you. I wish your
father were alive to see your game," she said.

I never know what to say when she talks about him.

"I wish he were too," I finally managed.

She took a sip of her tea. "Do you remember much
about him, Seth?"

I shook my head. "Sometimes I'll hear a man's voice,
and I'll think to myself that that's what he sounded like.
But other than his voice, I don't remember much. I wish
I did, but I don't.

She smiled sadly. "You were the world to him, Seth.
When you were a newborn, you'd wake up crying night
after night at three in the morning. You'd get fed, but
you couldn't get back to sleep. Your father would lie
down next to your crib, stick his hand up between the
slats, and you'd latch on to one of his fingers as if it
were a life preserver. That was the only thing that would

183

soothe you. Morning after morning I'd find him asleep with your hand tight around his finger." She paused. "He was a good man, Seth."

"I know he was, Mom."

She slowly shook her head. "No, you don't. Not really. You can't know a man from photographs or stories. You were robbed of your father, Seth. Death took him from you. Nothing will ever change that."

She stood, gave me a kiss, and returned to bed.

I stayed up a little longer, sitting in the kitchen and thinking. Actually, I didn't do much thinking: I felt. I felt the hole in me, the great emptiness inside me that should have been filled by my father. All around that hole were good things. My mother. Jimmy. School. Baseball. Day in and day out, those good things kept me from thinking about that hole, from feeling it. But it was always there.

14♦

Sunday morning dragged. Every minute was an hour. I thought I'd feel better when I reached the ballpark, but I didn't. Nobody did. We were grim-faced.

Sharront called us all together. "You may never get a chance to play in a game this big again." He looked us over. "Enjoy it," he said, a smile breaking out across his face. "Enjoy every minute of it."

On the field, I kept sneaking peeks at Steve Cannon. I had this feeling, this premonition. Cannon would come in as a reliever with the bases loaded in the last inning, and it would be up to me to get a hit off him to win the game.

Time had crawled, crawled. Then suddenly it raced. Maxwell led off the first with a looping single to left. I bunted him to second. Jimmy, first-pitch swinging, doubled him home. Todd ripped a single to right scoring Jimmy. Pacheco pounded what should have been a double-play grounder to third, but St. Francis's fielder threw the ball away. Tupo sliced a triple down the right-field line and scored on a wild pitch. By the time Johnson popped up for the third out, we had five runs on the scoreboard. I don't know who was more shocked, the St. Francis guys coming in to bat or us going out to field.

Their leadoff hitter smacked Russell's first pitch for a single right up the middle. The next guy banged a grounder into the hole. Jimmy dived, flat out, and snared the ball in the web of his glove. In a flash he was up firing to me. "Out!" the umpire yelled as I pivoted and fired to first. The hitter must have been trotting down the line, certain that his ball was headed to the outfield, because there was no way we should have turned two. But we did. The next batter popped up and our five-run lead was intact.

Maxwell led off the second with another hit, this time a double to right center. When I stepped in I figured I'd drag a bunt toward second. If I got a hit, great. If not, at least I'd have gotten Maxwell to third. The pitch came, a curve on the outside. I pushed it past the mound. The second baseman charged, bare-handed the ball, and fired to first, nipping me by half a step. But Maxwell

185

took third, and he scored when Jimmy lifted a fly to left center.

St. Francis got a couple runners on base in the bottom of the second. But with two on and two out, Todd made a nice running catch on a line drive to left center. The catch didn't look as good as it was because of the great jump he got on the ball. Really great players make things look easy.

After that, the innings rolled by. Russell kept the ball down. We fielded well and kept hitting. Two more runs in the fourth, one in the sixth. Steve Cannon pitched the top of the seventh and struck out the side. But heading to the bottom of the seventh we were up 9–1.

St. Francis's leadoff man hit a weak grounder toward me. I played it on two hops, tossed the ball to first. One down. Their next hitter worked the count to 3-2, then skied a high pop behind the plate that Johnson caught. I looked over at Jimmy. Even then — with two out and an eight-run lead — I couldn't believe the victory would come so easily. Jimmy gave me a little smile, held up two fingers. Russell went into his windup, delivered. The St. Francis guy sent a routine grounder to short. Jimmy gobbled it up, fired to first. We'd done it! Not only had we beaten St. Francis, we'd annihilated them!

We celebrated in the locker room like we'd clinched the championship. And why not? We were up one game with two games left, and those games were against the weakest teams in the league. Besides, we had to win only one of those games. If we finished in a tie with St. Francis, we'd go to the state tournament since we'd beaten them twice in the regular season.

186

So we hollered and laughed. Sharront came in, told us the season wasn't over. But even he must have felt we had it wrapped up, because he couldn't keep a stern look on his face. A couple of guys sneaked behind him and pushed him into the shower. Everybody cheered then, and Sharront laughed as he let the water drench his clothes.

15♦

In the middle of the night, the phone started ringing. I looked at my clock. It was 1:38. I covered my head with a pillow. The phone rang and rang and rang.

Finally I staggered to the kitchen, answered it.

"Is that you, Seth?"

The voice on the line was tense.

"Yeah, it's me. Who is this?"

"Alex."

"Alex," I said sleepily. "What do you want?"

"Listen, Seth. Jimmy's been in an accident."

I woke up fast. "What?"

"He's been in an accident. He's at Sequoia Hospital."

"Say that again."

"We were up at Huddart Park. Jimmy left maybe an hour before Dan and me. Right after he left, we heard a siren, but we didn't think anything of it. Anyway, when we were driving home we saw his Camaro piled into a tree off Kings Mountain Road. The police were there. Dan didn't stop because . . . well, you know . . . he just

187

couldn't. I called Sequoia Hospital a minute ago, and they said Jimmy was there.''

"How badly is he hurt?'' I asked.

"They wouldn't tell me. But the Camaro didn't look all that smashed up. It wasn't totaled or anything.'' Alex paused. "Listen, Seth, I've got to get off the phone. My parents might wake up and I don't want them to know about any of this.''

"Wait a second, Alex,'' I said, but the phone had gone dead.

I rushed to my room, pulled on my clothes. Then I grabbed the keys to the car. Before I made it to the door, my mother came out of her room.

"I'm going to Sequoia Hospital,'' I said. "Jimmy has been in an accident.''

"What?'' she said groggily.

I couldn't wait. "I've got to go now, Mom. I'll be back as soon as I can.''

Driving to the hospital, I thought about Jimmy's future. If Sharront found out Jimmy had been drinking, he'd kick him off the team for good. The major-league scouts would hear about it, too. Would they want to draft some kid with a drinking problem? It didn't seem like it.

The whole ride I was racking my brain, trying to come up with some way to keep the truth from Sharront. But there wasn't any way. There just wasn't. The doctors were sure to take a blood sample. They'd find alcohol in his blood, and they'd call the school. It might even make the newspaper.

Then another, scarier, thought came to me. What if

188

Jimmy smashed up his leg or his arm so badly he couldn't play anymore? Then what would happen to him? Baseball was the only thing that mattered to him. The only thing.

I parked my car and ran into the emergency room. I looked around, trying to find someone to talk to. The place seemed deserted. Then, down a long hall, I saw Sharront with Jimmy's mother. *He knows*, I thought to myself. *He already knows.* I felt my stomach sink. Sharront had his arm around Jimmy's mother. They were walking toward me. I raised my hand in a kind of half-wave, but neither of them noticed. Jimmy's mother's head was bowed, and her hand was covering her eyes. Sharront was looking down too. He was about ten feet away when he finally looked up.

Tears were streaming down his face.

In that instant I knew.

I knew that being kicked off the team was nothing; that the state tournament was nothing; that the major leagues are nothing; that baseball is nothing.

Sharront drew even with me. He put his hands on my shoulders. "Jimmy is dead," he whispered. Then he turned back to Mrs. Winter. The two of them continued down the corridor and disappeared into a room.

I couldn't stay in that white, white hallway. The bright lights were blinding me. The walls were pressing in, the ceiling was pressing down. I ran out of the hospital, out into the black night.

There's a little park across from Sequoia Hospital. I made my way there, slumped onto a bench. I can't even say I thought. My mind was too paralyzed to think. I

189

sat. I sat there the rest of the night looking at the stars. That's not even right. I sat looking at the black between the stars.

I didn't want the sun to come up. But the universe didn't care what I wanted. Night slowly gave way to dawn. Little birds started hopping in the trees; lights went on in the houses around the park. I had to go home.

When I stood I realized how cold I was, how stiff I was. I hobbled over to the car, started it up. It was then that I got the shakes. They must have lasted for two or three minutes. And the shakes didn't go away all at once either. But when they finally did, I leaned my head forward against the steering wheel and cried for Jimmy Winter.

16✦

The funeral service was Wednesday, the day we should have been clinching the league title. My mother and I sat in the back row of the church. They had Jimmy up front in an open shiny silver casket. The expression on his face was all wrong. Jimmy was intense, always staring out from those green eyes. The Jimmy in the casket looked peaceful. He was never that way.

The minister started by talking about what a tragedy it was, a young life lost and all that. Then he got on to the problems of teenagers, and how God might have had Jimmy die so other kids might learn, and how it might actually be for the better.

I wanted to scream.

190

After the funeral service at the church, I dropped my mother off at our house, then drove out alone to the cemetery in Colma. I had to see him go into the ground. Fewer people were at the graveside service. Alex, Todd, Dan Hill, and maybe eight or ten adults. Mr. Winter came over to me while the minister was talking. Somehow Mr. Winter seemed taller, stronger than ever. "He was a good boy, wasn't he?" he whispered. I nodded. We stood, side by side, for a few moments. "Did Jimmy ever call you?" I asked.

Mr. Winter looked puzzled.

"He was going to ask you to come to a game. Did he ever do it?"

"No," Mr. Winter replied, "he didn't."

"He wanted to," I said. "I know he did."

Mr. Winter squeezed my elbow, then moved back up to the front.

Jimmy's mother broke down when they lowered the casket into the ground. So did Sharront, so did Alex and Todd and Dan Hill. So did everyone but me. I don't know why, but I didn't.

After the service was over, I sat down under a tree and waited. I didn't know what I was waiting for, but I knew I was waiting for something.

As I sat there, I tried to string words together in my head that would say what Jimmy meant to me. I thought that if I could string them together, I could remember them, and so I'd be sure to always remember him. I thought about coming back from L.A. and meeting him for the first time. I thought about John Tustin. I thought about drinking beer at Todd's house, about turning

191

double plays, about Wiffle ball, about the pitching machine at Tom Wells, about making the varsity. I added all those things up — and a thousand other things, too — but the sum wasn't right. They didn't add up to Jimmy. They didn't come close. He was my friend. It's the only word I have for him.

One hour passed, and then another. Finally they came. The men with the shovels. I watched them fill the hole in the ground with dirt, good clean dirt. I heard the dirt land on the coffin, over and over. Then the sound became softer, muffled. For an instant I didn't know why it sounded different. Then I understood. The dirt wasn't hitting the coffin anymore. Jimmy was under the earth.

17♦

There was a team meeting the next day. The situation was pretty simple. We'd forfeited the Wednesday game. The question was whether to forfeit Sunday's game too and give the title to St. Francis. Sharront said it was up to us. "If anybody has anything to say, say it now. Then we'll vote. Whichever way it comes out, I want the whole team to stick to it."

Todd stood. "I say we play. It's what Jimmy would have wanted." Around the locker room guys murmured agreement.

"Anybody else?" Sharront asked. The room fell silent. Sharront looked at me. "Seth, you want to say something?"

I could feel my teammates' eyes on me. And why not? I was Jimmy's oldest friend, his best friend. They
192

wanted to hear how I felt. But I didn't know how I felt. I shook my head.

There were twenty-one of us on the team, but the vote was 18–0 to play. Two other guys besides me left their ballots blank.

"That's it then," Sharront said. "No practices this week. Be at San Carlos at eleven."

When I entered the locker room Sunday morning, Sharront handed me a black armband. "Let's win this thing for Jimmy," he said. I tried to answer, but all I managed was a little nod of the head.

As the guys dressed, nobody spoke above a whisper. The loudest sounds were the cleats against the cement floor and the opening and closing of the lockers. Right before we took the field, Sharront clapped his hands. "Okay, gentlemen. Time to put everything else aside. Let's concentrate on baseball."

That I could do. I couldn't make sense out of Jimmy's death, or out of whether we should or shouldn't be playing the game — but I could concentrate on baseball.

The strange thing about warming up for the game was that everything was so ordinary. Jimmy's death didn't change the sound of a ball being hit by a bat. Jimmy's death didn't change the way I fielded grounders, or the way outfielders chased down fly balls.

But when the game began, when I took Jimmy's spot at shortstop — that was different. I *knew,* I positively *knew* where Jimmy would have positioned himself for each batter. And I took my own position a little to the right, or to the left, or up or back. I couldn't bring myself

193

to stand in the exact spot where Jimmy would have stood. I just couldn't.

The game should have been a blowout. San Carlos didn't have much hitting, and Russell had his best stuff, so he breezed through their lineup. And their pitcher was no great shakes. Todd doubled home a run in the first, and after that we had runners on base all game. One clutch hit would have blown it wide open.

But that big hit never came. We stranded two runners in the second; we left the bases loaded in the third. In the fifth we had runners at second and third with nobody out and still couldn't push home a run. I worked a lead-off walk in the sixth, but got no farther than second.

Russell retired San Carlos in order in the bottom of the sixth, but he was tiring. Batters he'd struck out earlier were catching up with his fastball. All they managed were long fly balls that inning, but it was a bad sign. Sharront had Radinsky up and warming.

"Let's get some runs!" Sharront screamed as we came in for the top of the seventh. "Let's go!"

But we didn't. A pop-up, a ground out, a lazy fly to right. It was the first time in the game we'd gone down in order.

As I grabbed my glove and headed to shortstop for the bottom of the seventh, a sense of doom came over me. We held a 1–0 lead. Three more outs and the championship was ours. But I didn't think we'd make it. We'd dedicated the game to Jimmy — and we were going to lose.

When you're tired, you sometimes try too hard. That's what happened to Russell. He overthrew the first pitch.

It sailed inside, plunking the San Carlos batter in the back and putting the tying run on first.

Sharront came out. "Nice game," he said. Then he called for Radinsky.

The first hitter Radinsky faced bounced a little two-hopper to Duncan. We got the force at second, but the ball wasn't hit hard enough to turn the double play. The second out came on the next pitch — the batter lifted a little pop-up behind the plate and Johnson hauled it in.

We were close, so close. Still that sense of doom hung over me.

The hitter stepped in. Radinsky missed with two curveballs, and the batter drove the third pitch on a line into right field. Maxwell fielded the ball cleanly, but then lost his head. Instead of throwing the ball to second, he tried to gun down the lead runner at third. The throw was way late, and the batter took second. The winning run was in scoring position.

Radinsky looked in to the bench. Sharront held up four fingers to signal an intentional walk. It made baseball sense. By loading the bases, we set up a force play at every base. But there was a risk, too, because with the bases loaded a walk would force in the tying run.

San Carlos's coach called back the scheduled batter and sent up a pinch hitter, the littlest guy on the team. He couldn't have been more than five two. And when he stepped in, he crouched as low as he could in the batter's box.

Radinsky's first pitch was high, and the next one was about a foot outside. On the 2-0 pitch, the batter showed bunt. It was 100 percent fake, but Radinsky flinched a little, and his pitch bounced up to the plate. Three balls and no strikes.

Radinsky turned his back on home plate and looked out toward me. For a second I couldn't figure why. Then it came to me. It was Jimmy he wanted to see. It was Jimmy who would have given him confidence.

I felt a lump rise in my throat. *Why not?* I thought. *Why not?*

So I did what Jimmy would have done. I hustled in to talk to Radinsky. "Forget about the batter," I said, doing my best to sound calm. "Just hit Johnson's glove."

Radinsky nodded. "Okay, Seth."

I returned to my position.

Radinsky went into his windup, delivered. "Strike one!" the ump yelled. Johnson tossed the ball back. Radinsky rubbed it up, stepped back on the rubber, fired. "Strike two!" the ump yelled.

It was then I moved a half-step toward second base. That's all. A half-step. But by moving that half-step I was positioned exactly where Jimmy would have been.

Radinsky delivered another fastball, only this time the batter swung away, sending a hard ground ball up the middle. I was off with the crack of the bat. The first hop was just short of the mound, the second near the bag. I dived, stretching as far as I could. The ball caught in the web of my glove. I scrambled to my feet and fired to first. The umpire raised his thumb. "You're out!" he bellowed.

We'd won. We were the champions.

We started to celebrate. The whole team — outfielders, infielders, the guys on the bench — all of us raced to the pitcher's mound. We even managed a few screams of joy before we remembered. Then we looked at one another and suddenly we didn't know what to do. The cheers died in our throats. We were all there, in the center of the diamond, and for a moment we were all quiet.

We'd said we were playing for Jimmy, but we'd really played for ourselves. We'd wanted to pretend that death doesn't happen, that everything just goes on and on. And maybe someday we would be able to pretend. But not then, not at that moment. Jimmy had the heart of a champion, not us. It was his championship, not ours.

Sharront broke the spell. "It's over, gentlemen," he said. "It's over."

18♦

Santa Rosa High knocked us out of the state tournament. The final was 11–3. They scored five times in the first inning off Alex Furmin, and they kept hammering against Willis and Radinsky. But it wasn't pitching that did us in. We just didn't have anything left to give. It was a relief to have the season end.

On the last Monday before school let out, a woman came to talk to the team about Jimmy. Afterward Coach Sharront made me go to the counselor's office to talk to her one-on-one. "Don't keep things bottled up," she said. "Tell me what you're thinking."

But I couldn't tell her what I was thinking. How could I tell her what I was thinking when I didn't even know

197

myself? So she talked some more, and I sat some more. Finally she let me go.

I skipped the awards banquet. I don't know how any of the guys on the team could go, but some of them did. They voted me "Most Improved." Sharront brought the trophy over. It's sitting in my closet right now. I couldn't bring myself to put it on the mantel. Maybe someday I will.

I pretty much stayed in my room through June and July. I didn't get my job back at the golf course; I didn't hit balls at Tom Wells. I didn't do anything.

Then, at the start of August, my mother came into my room. "Seth Barham, you can't brood forever. You've got to get on with your own life." Her voice was firm, almost angry.

"I'm not brooding," I shot right back. And to prove it, I went to the movies that night. But as I sat alone in the dark, all I thought about was death — Jimmy's, my father's, my own. That's when it hit me that I had to get a grip on what had happened, just like a second baseman has got to get a grip on a baseball before he can throw a runner out at first.

I remembered something that woman had told me. "You might try writing it down," she'd said as I was leaving. "Sometimes by writing things down you can understand them better. And once you understand them, you can put them behind you. You can go on."

So that's what I've done. I've written it down. And now that I'm finished, I'm not sure whether she was right or not. I'm not sure whether I do have a grip on what happened to Jimmy, or whether I'll ever put it behind me, any more than I'll ever put my father's death behind me.

Take this very minute. It's a Saturday afternoon. I'm looking out the window. The leaves are rustling in the trees, and I'm thinking that I should be on a ball field right now, that I should be standing at second base and Jimmy should be standing at shortstop, that he should toss some dirt in the air, watch the wind take it, and then tell me to be careful on pop flies. And I should nod to him, then look up in the stands. And I'm thinking my father should be sitting there, and that my father should nod to me, too, and maybe give me a little secret smile, a smile that only he and I share. And I'm thinking the sun should be shining on that ball field, and on Jimmy and on my father and on me.